THE CHRISTMAS SECRET

An Atlantic Canadian
Christmas Reader

Edited by Dan Soucoup

NIMBUS
PUBLISHING LTD

Christmas Traditions

Introduction

Dan Soucoup

Almost everyone has unique memories surrounding the Christmas season. Stories, recollections, and family traditions all characterize what's best about the holidays and many vivid reminiscences go back to our childhood in the month of December. My strongest Christmas memories go back to 1959, and like those of many Canadian boys, they involve hockey.

Winter had come early that year and the ice was hard on the ponds and backyard rinks around Parkton, New Brunswick. It was a hockey-mad time and on Second Avenue, Peter Doiron's dad had built a large outdoor rink. It was big news in the north end of Moncton, and the neighbourhood kids all wanted to play on the Doiron rink.

Paul's father worked at the CN shops with my dad, and a few days before Christmas he mentioned that I could come over on Boxing Day and play on Peter's team. I had been given new skates for Christmas and the excitement of playing organized hockey on the new rink was almost overwhelming.

December 26 was crisp and frosty when I headed across First Avenue with my new skates already laced. When I got to the Doiron house, the rink was already buzzing with players warming up and spectators standing behind the boards. Peter wore a Montréal Canadiens uniform he had received for Christmas and it had a big "C," for captain, stitched on it. I had my faded red jersey on, and I could tell our team's players because we all were wearing red sweaters.

Soon the whistle went and we started to play, although I was on the bench, relegated to the second line. Peter's dad was coaching our team and pretty soon he signalled to some of the boys to come off the ice and catch a break. My chance had finally come and I quickly jumped down and skated over to play left wing. The puck was dropped and we were away. Peter quickly got the puck and passed it over. I moved in towards the net with only one defenceman back. This was what I had dreamed about.

And then it happened. I tried to shoot the puck, but my stick somehow got stuck on the boards and my blade broke— clean off. I skated off the ice in shock, and since there were no spare sticks, I left the rink in disgust and shuffled on my skates back home. My first chance to play real hockey was over.

When I got home, Dad asked me what happened and just laughed when I told him, almost in tears, that I was off the team because I had no stick. He disappeared into the basement and came back up with a brand new stick and a roll of tape.

"I made this out of some dried birch I had around for your birthday next month but I guess you need a stick now," he said with a smile, taping up the blade and passing it over to me. I jumped with joy as I realized I was back in action, and quickly ran to the rink as hard as I could. I was soon back on the bench and eager to play. Coach Doiron chuckled as he saw me sitting there again. But soon he motioned for me to get back out on the ice, and I was away.

I was barely ten years old and delighted with myself. It was the best Christmas ever! I had avoided disaster and, with my father's Boxing Day surprise, had also managed to get an extra Christmas present while surviving my first official hockey game.

❦

This splendid collection of Christmas stories and memories from throughout Atlantic Canada features some of our region's greatest storytellers. From charming tales by Antonine Maillet, Dan Ross, and Bob Kroll, to heartfelt holiday stories by Wayne Curtis, Will R. Bird, Michael O. Nowlan, and David Weale, these works represent the very best of East Coast seasonal fiction, and are wonderful keepsakes for Christmas reading.

And it wouldn't be Christmas without nostalgic memories recalling past Christmastimes, including contributions by well-known writers such as Alden Nowlan, Linden MacIntyre, Gary L. Saunders, Evelyn M. Richardson, Norman Creighton, Helen Fogwill Porter, and Lesley Choyce. Other talented writers who have contributed to these precious recollections of Christmases past throughout Atlantic Canada include Alistair Cameron, Stanley T. Spicer, Nellie P. Strowbridge, Phyllis R. Blakeley, Trudy Duivenvoorden Mitic, and the delightful Andy MacDonald, whose story about growing up poor at Christmastime in Cape Breton truly defines the concept of celebrating the holidays "on a shoestring."

So pull up a chair and get good and comfortable. It's probably going to get cold outside, or perhaps threaten to snow. These stories will do much to warm the heart, even on the coldest days.

All the houses would light up and pretty soon the whole village looked like a big Christmas tree. Normally about that time we'd be giving the kids a good licking to get them to bed, but not that night. That night we'd have to give them a licking to keep them up. Yes, we would. It was the only night of the year the little buggers couldn't wait to get to bed, because of Santa Claus, who wouldn't come down the chimley until they was fast asleep. Now it must've been someone else's kids who put that idea into their heads, but anyways they believed it. Didn't matter how much breath we wasted telling them that Santa Claus couldn't possibly know where it was we lived, and that anyways we didn't even have a chimley...they didn't want to hear nothing about that, they'd just drop off to sleep in our arms while we was talking to them.

But they'd wake up soon enough once Noume cranked up his old grammerphone. We'd all get together over at Don the Moose's place, and that's when Noume'd bring out his grammerphone that he brought back with him from Overseas, and which there's some who try to say that no one gave it to him, either, the grammerphone, but then they'd have the Moose to deal with, who'd tell them he'd given them something to remember him by if they didn't shut their traps. So then we'd all get out our records and crank up the grammerphone, and oh, there'd be Willy Lamotte and La Bolduc and "It's a Long Way to Tipperary."

At eleven o'clock, any of us who could still stand upright went to church for midnight Mass. We'd go a bit early so as to get a good place. Not a place to sit, of course, there weren't enough pews to go around, but they'd let us stand in the back at the end of the centre aisle, because it was Christmas. We couldn't hear the priest say mass because there wasn't room for us in the pews, but we could see the parade when it come in through the back of the church. The priest all done up in his best rig: cassocks and soutanes and so many surplices piled on him you wouldn't think he'd know what to do with them all. And all done up in convent lace. And behind him the younger priests, and then the Children of Mary, then the choirboys carrying the Wax-Baby-Jesus on a pole, all done up in a beautiful lace gown and his hair all curled. They'd take him over to the stable and set him down by the mare and the bull.

You need not to worry about the Wax-Baby-Jesus' white gown, because the stable didn't smell like a real stable. It didn't have manure in it or nothing like that, I would have noticed something like that. No, it had a nice crib made of good, clean cardboard with a nice blue silk blanket onto it, and nice, clean straw made from excelcis, and the animals were all stuffed and shaved, like. There wasn't no smell of sheep or the barn or nothing like that, except maybe coming from us. We didn't smell all that good, I can tell you, which is another reason we kept in the back. We didn't have lacy clothes or our hair all done up. We could've stood in the crèche ourselves, alongside of the shepherds—that would've been something to see!

Normally we'd leave the church just before the sermon. Not that the priest gave a bad sermon or nothing. He had a voice on him could be heard all the way down the end of the bay, if he wanted it to. But he never raised his voice for midnight Mass, practically whispered his sermon to the people sitting in the front pews, he was that moved. The rest of us couldn't hear a damn thing he said. And anyways we didn't want to wait and leave with them others because we didn't want to be noticed, like. So usually somewhere between "O Holy Night" and "While Shepherds Washed Their Flocks by Night" we'd sneak on out the front door and go home and finish of Christmas in our own place.

The barn scrapings was real there, I can tell you, and the straw, too. And maybe if we had ourselves a shining star to hang on our door the three wise men might've made a mistake and brought their coal and Frankenstein to us instead. But they never showed up. No one did. Christmas for us was like the Bingo or the Irving store: we didn't play and we didn't pay, we just watched other people playing and paying, just like we watched the Wax-Baby-Jesus getting carried straight to his manger, and us, we got to go straight home, same as always.

What if maybe one Christmas the parade took a wrong turn and ended up here at our place, all the shepherds and the wise men and the camels and Joseph and Mary and the little Wax-Baby-Jesus, the whole Holy Family with all the angels and archangels and the mare and the bull, what if they all got lost one Christmas and came here by mistake...wouldn't that be something to see?

Maybe Elisabeth-à-Zacharias would appear before us from the hills of Sainte-Marie to tell us that one of her nieces was about to have a baby. And we'd run around cleaning the place up, getting the old cradle down from the Saint's attic, making a blanket out of an old comforter. We'd get everything all prepared, ready to receive the baby. Then we'd wait. We'd wait for the angels to come down and sing "Gloria in excelsior day-glo" out on the bay to tell everyone that unto us a child is born in one of the shacks down on the south shore.

And then all the fishermen would come out of their caplin shacks, and the poor would emerge from their hovels, along with the Saint and the Moose and the Jug and me and Gapi, and we'd send for Sarah Bidoche the midwife to be here in case something went wrong. But nothing would go wrong, because everything would take place as it says in the Scriptures, like in a miracle. And we'd go back in to see the Baby Jesus in his mother's arms and Joseph strutting about like he was the father, which they out he was, or sitting on the flour barrel, with the mare and the bull breathing on the crib to keep it warm. And the wise men would be kneeling in front of him with their presents, only this time they'd be real presents, not coal or myrtle or whatever but something a kid could use, children's toys like a teddy bear or a top that plays Christmas carols when it spins.

We'd be right at home in our shacks and wouldn't be at all embarrassed to take our places among the shepherds and the camels. I'm pretty sure Don the Moose would find something to talk to Joseph and the wise men about. Maybe Gapi would sit down with the menfolk and pass his tobacco pouch over to Zacharias. Yes, I can see that happening. I always thought Zacharias and Gapi had a lot in common; he didn't put his trust in just anyone, did he, and you couldn't make him change his mind about a thing. Yes sir, he and Gapi would look good sitting on the same bench.

And I can see the Jug going over to have a few quiet words with the Holy Virgin, telling her things, you know, things she wasn't ever able to tell the priest. Or maybe she wouldn't say nothing, maybe they'd just sit there, and they'd laugh together, the two of them, as they looked down at the baby.

And then we'd send for Noume with his grammerphone and records. And Gerard-à-Jos would bring his juice harp. And we'd all sing a few dirges, or maybe "It's a Long Way to Tipperary."

Of course, the Saint would have to join in and sprinkle her vinegar over the whole thing. She might even take it into her head to take a picture of the Holy Family, tell the wise men to stand on either side of the cradle, get all the shepherds down on one knee. One thing's for sure, she'd never see Christmas the same as the rest of us, not her, not the Saint.

Well, and maybe she's got a good point, too. If the procession ever took a wrong turn and ended up down in our part of town, it wouldn't really be Christmas at all, would it, because we couldn't properly tart up the front of our shacks with crêpe paper and coloured lights. And we don't have all them bells and stars and gewgaws and plastic Santa Clauses or papier-mâché crèches made to look like rocks so you can't tell the difference. No, we wouldn't know how to receive the Baby Jesus into our homes, would we, not without all that lace and silk blankets and fine crinkly paper for making fake straw. Nope, we don't have nothing to make a nice Nativity Scene out of.

A fine Christmas like that, it wasn't meant for the likes of us.

Jeff looked up into the kind face of the old man, and the smile that crossed his young features was full of meaning and pride. Rising above the confusion and pain that had filled his puzzled, boyish mind was a new sense of understanding. A perception in itself, part of the change in life of which the mayor had spoken. The continuing pattern that would mark his growth to an adult. Now he would go back with Uncle Fred with the gnawing pain and doubts that had tormented him eased. Because he knew his father, his tree, and in a way even he, had given as generously as they could in the real spirit of Christmas.

The Gift

Bob Kroll

In this powerful narrative, set in Antigonish many years ago at Christmas Eve, the reader is taken on a hair-raising journey with old Annie Mullen, the remarkable Guardian of the Christ Child.

Some people have a gift for storytelling. My mother was one. She had more stories than a tin peddler had pots. She told ghost stories, love stories, fables, yarns, stories from the Bible, and stories about when she was a little girl. The family never tired of hearing them, and my mother never tired of telling.

One story she loved to tell was about the Guardian of the Christ Child. On Christmas Eve, for about as long as I can remember, after our throats had dried with singing and we had settled before the Christmas tree with mugs of hot cocoa, my mother would tell us about Annie Mullen, the Guardian of the Christ Child. My mother always prefaced the story by saying it had happened a long time ago, when she was eight or nine years old. She swore the story was true. By the way she told it, her voice strong with memory, I believed her. I still do. As best as I can remember, this is the story she told.

Annie Mullen whacked her thigh in a most unladylike fashion. She sucked her lips into a broad, toothless grin and let out a "whoop." Annie Mullen was eighty-five, and for the first time in her long hard life, luck had come her way.

Father Shea held up to the congregation the yellow paper with Annie's name on it. He had drawn it from a barrel that contained the names of just about every family in the parish. Father Shea was as happy as Annie, and most parishioners were too. They smiled and clapped and took turns calling congratulations across the church hall. Annie beamed at the attention and the parishioners beamed back. After all, at eighty-five, Annie would not have too many more chances to win the honour of carrying the statue of the Christ Child to church on Christmas Eve and placing it in the manger.

This was a time when people believed that God moved through the world and touched their lives and stirred their hearts with hope. This was a time when people believed that every living day was a gift from God, and that a prayer at night offered a humble "thanks" for His tender mercies. This was a time when people believed that the Guardian of the Christ Child was indeed an honour with a host of blessings descending upon the chosen household. The luck of the draw left the selection in the hands of God. So this Christmas, one could say that God had selected Annie Mullen to be this year's Guardian of the Christ Child.

Annie was all pins and needles waiting for Christmas Eve. She had her best black dress with the lace collar flat-ironed and laid out two whole days before the big occasion. She had crocheted a small comforter for the statue because the cold weather had set in, and to this she had pinned her dead husband's photograph so he could be with her and share in the honour.

Because Annie was alone now, she asked her neighbours and their six children to accompany her to church. The Connolly kids ranged in age from fifteen down to six. They were: Julia, Ellery, Sarah, Viola, Xavier, and Rebecca. Each one was more excited than the other, bubbling with anticipation of standing beside Annie when she laid the Christ Child in the manger. They could hardly talk about it without catching their breath and shivering all over. Mr. and Mrs. Connolly were excited too—and proud that Annie had chosen their children to be "her assistants."

And so when the snowstorm hit on the day before Christmas, Annie felt her spirits go numb with the blowing cold. So did the kids. All that day, they moped at the parlour window and watched the driven snow quickly close the roads. Travelling the five miles to church was now impossible. Only townsfolk would attend Christmas Eve service, and they must do so without the Guardian of the Christ Child.

About seven o'clock that evening, the Connolly kids and their parents trudged next door to Annie's house to make sure Annie had plenty of wood for a fire and a few days' food, because, as their father said, this storm "could blow into a blizzard." They also wanted to console Annie that her turn as the Guardian of the Christ Child would keep well enough for next Christmas Eve.

They sat by the black cook stove in Annie's kitchen with their chins on their chests and sadness hanging from their faces. They drank tea, ate Christmas cookies, and talked about anything to help pass the unhappiest Christmas Eve they had ever spent.

About nine o'clock, as their mother was about to say that the hour had come for them to return home, the train to Sydney, Cape Breton, blew its whistle for a crossing. Julia cocked an ear as the train whistle blew for another crossing a few miles down the line. Her eyes widened as an idea shaped itself into words.

"We can walk the tracks into town," Julia said.

Then Ellery jumped up and cried even louder: "The train just cleared 'em! We can walk the tracks!"

Mrs. Connolly slowly raised her head at the thought of it. A second thought, however, squeezed her face into a frown: "What about Annie?"

But old Annie Mullen was faster than that. She was already out the kitchen door and back, dragging a belly-bumper sled with a box on top. She used it for hauling firewood from the shed. She chewed her lips into a smile. The Connollys could walk the tracks into town, all right, and haul Annie Mullen, the Guardian of the Christ Child, on the belly-bumper sled.

So they did, with Mr. Connolly leading the way, and all six kids and Mrs. Connolly taking turns pushing and pulling the sled. They slipped on the rails and stumbled over the ties, laughing at the fun of it and singing Christmas carols into the blowing wind.

They had travelled three miles when they came to the trestle bridge. They did not dare cross in the snow-blind darkness for fear of falling between the ties and into the icy river below. Snow gathered on their stocking caps and slumped shoulders and on Annie, who sat cramped in the wooden box on the sled, cradling the statue under her heavy woollen coat. Disappointment filled their eyes. They stood there for the longest time, unsure of what to do, unwilling to concede defeat.

All at once, Annie Mullen groped her way out of the wooden box and held up the statue wrapped in the crocheted comforter, as though to show the Christ Child and photo of her dead husband the obstacle that stood in their way. Then she waddled forward just as sure-footed as an old goat on a rocky ledge. Without even thinking about it, the others followed close behind, careful to match each step to Annie's footprints.

They arrived at church in time for Christmas Eve service. Annie had the seat of honour, the high-back chair beside the nativity scene. Throughout the service, she cradled the Christ Child in her lap. She was so proud, proud for herself and for the children, and for her dead husband whose photo was still pinned to the small crocheted comforter.

As the choir sang "Silent Night," Annie rose from the chair. Julia, Ellery, Sarah, Viola, Xavier, and Rebecca rose with her. All together they placed the Christ Child in the manger. They faced the congregation and joined in the singing. Once again Annie Mullen chewed her lips into a broad grin, folded her arms on her chest, and hugged herself—the Guardian of the Christ Child.

After mass, as they stood around the nativity scene, Father Shea insisted that Annie and the Connollys stay the night at the rectory. He would not have them returning home in such a storm. And he would certainly not have them risking their lives again by crossing that slippery bridge in the dark. Why they had crossed it in the first place was beyond good sense.

Mr. and Mrs. Connolly agreed. Venturing out in a winter storm was foolish indeed, and crossing the trestle bridge was even more foolish than that.

"But when we heard the train whistle," Mrs. Connolly explained to Father Shea, "walking the tracks just seemed the right thing to do."

"I don't know why we crossed the bridge," Mr. Connolly added, "but...well...Annie just looked so sure of herself...We just had to follow."

The children agreed. All had felt as though something had been guiding Annie across the trestle bridge. Father Shea turned to Annie with a confused and curious look on his face—the kind of look that begged an explanation.

Annie settled back into the seat of honour and folded her lips into a smile. "My husband and me crossed that bridge a zillion times on our way into town. And tonight, I just needed him to show me where to step."

Granny's Art

Will R. Bird

*In this heartwarming Yuletide story from Angel Cove,
a young Newfoundland teacher on her first assignment
in a small outport village becomes storm-stayed over
the holidays, and learns the true meaning of Christmas.*

It was cold and windy weather when Simon Cotter rapped at Abel Harmon's door and asked if they could take Granny for a month. She had been with Peleg Filler for four weeks and it was someone else's turn. "Bring her right over," said Bride. "I've seen her a few times and I think she's a dear."

"And from what I've heard," said Abel, "I'd much rather have her than the schoolteacher. Eli Torrent took her and he says she's uppity no end. The way he talks, I imagine she'll have idees about goin' to St. John's for Crissmus."

The cold increased at Angel Cove and there were snow flurries almost every day. Everyone wrapped warmly to go to the store and wives began counting every dollar over and over before making a purchase. Brooks were frozen over and ice formed along the shore. Jake Holder had the job of making the fire in the schoolhouse stove, and he had it almost red-hot an hour and a half before the teacher arrived. She was from

St. John's and her name was Millicent Rand. Eli Torrent reported that she wrote three or four letters a week and thought there would be a mailboat running regularly.

The weather became colder and colder until there was a December morning when Millicent could see her breath as she roused and raised on an elbow.

Plunk! Plunk! Plunk! Three sharp blows on the stovepipe, close up to the kitchen ceiling. "Eight o'clock, miss." Eli Torrent's booming outdoor voice seemed to rattle things.

"Coming!" called Millicent. She slid her feet to the floor, snatched an armload of clothing from the chair beside the bed, and hurried over to the stovepipe to dress. As she pulled off her bed socks she heard Eli, in the kitchen below, sit down at the table. He had heard the squeak of the floor as she crossed it, and so knew that the teacher was "up."

Millicent's light yellow hair was sleep-fluffed and a sleep flush deepened the colour of her cheeks, but a hasty glance into the mirror of the imitation oak bureau did not seem to put her in good spirits, despite the beauty she saw there. She discarded the biggest secret in the Cove, her pyjamas, and shivered into woollens. If there were colder places than Angel Cove in December, she did not believe they were inhabited.

"Is teacher up yet?" It was a childish treble that sounded up the stovepipe, and it was immediately hushed. Millicent was interested. If little Mary was so quickly silenced, there must be a reason, and the sooner she was downstairs the better. It might be something important, as when Tom Holder broke an oar and drifted to the headrocks in the bay, and was capsized and almost drowned.

Eli had finished his breakfast when she was downstairs. "It's snappy cold this morning," he remarked, as if giving news. "It snowed a foot last night."

Mrs. Eli, a washed-out-looking woman, the still, small voice of the family, seemed waiting for something, and when Eli did not speak further, she looked at him. "Tell her now," she said. "Soon over is best."

Millicent sensed disaster. "What is it?" she asked quickly.

"Simon Cotter brought word that the boat ain't comin'."

Crash! Calamity in one terse sentence! "'The boat ain't comin'."

Millicent moved her lips twice before she could make them whisper, "Why?"

"Too late. That was all the word they got at the Point," boomed Eli, as if he were glad it was no fault of his. "Four years the boat didn't come."

"But—but," Millicent's first weakening horror was giving way to baffled, angry feelings, "why didn't they send word before? I'd have stopped school a month earlier, sooner—soon than stay frozen in here over Christmas."

"It's bad," agreed Eli in an exasperating manner. "There's no other way down along 'cept you go by dog team, an' nobody's goin' now."

Millicent shivered despairingly. What wretched luck! At Angel Cove for Christmas! And after bolstering her courage for weeks with the thought that she'd be home then!

"Sit down and have a cup of tea," begged Mrs. Eli. "You won't get warm till you're warm inside. We'll make some sort of Christmas for you, and you'll be able to get down after New Year's."

After New Year's! What a remote time to look ahead!

Millicent drank the hot tea coloured with tinned milk, and accepted a portion of baked cod with her toast and molasses. She shuddered as she surveyed the table, the cheap white cloth bordered with red flowers, the wooden-handled knives and forks, the plate of fish. Fish! Cod and salmon, cod tongues, cod heads, cod, cod, more cod, always cod—baked, boiled, and fried. Cod, cod, cod. How she hated fish, the sight of it, the smell of it, the taste of it. Only the fact that she was young and healthy and with good appetite enabled her to swallow her food at all. The house, the people, everything, seemed suddenly to have become permeated with fish.

She finished eating and pushed away from the table, conscious that Mrs. Eli was dismayed by her petulant manner. But she could not help it, and she pulled a heavy roll-neck sweater over her head and enveloped herself in a thick blanket coat before she could nod to the woman with forced cheerfulness.

"All set, Mary," she said to the sturdy ten-year-old, and followed her into a swirl of fine snow.

It was only a short way to the school, but Millicent thought of a thousand things before she reached it. Vague, but dominant, was the idea that she, in some way she could not define, had been tricked. All Angel Cove, she was sure, knew she had planned to reach home in time for Christmas—home in St. John's, a big comfortable house that did not smell of fish, a home of soft beds and comfortable furniture. Why, then, had they allowed fate to foil her?

Ten eager boys and nine anxious girls were around the big stove in the centre of the schoolroom, and they watched her entry with bated breath. Millicent knew they were trying to gauge her attitude before they spoke of that which would now be common knowledge in the Cove. Somehow, their watchfulness was irritating. "Kitty Holder," she flared, "wipe your nose, and you too, Angela Filler. Boys, go to the door and shake yourselves. You're melting all over the floor."

"Yes, teacher." "All right, teacher." The same grave-voiced respect from both sexes. Millicent felt helpless, stifled. It was as if the Cove were blockading everything she wished. Tears stung near the surface as she rang the bell and called the roll in a shrill, mechanical voice.

It was the last day of school before Christmas holidays began, and she had intended to be very gracious, but the room and its occupants seemed to have become alien to her. She could not look pleasant, and not a child dared whisper. Recess came, and the scholars grouped stiffly near the door, staring at the frost-trimmed windows and glancing covertly at her. She laughed suddenly, catchily; she had to laugh for fear of crying.

"Come," she called. "I'm feeling all right now. Come and tell me what you'd like best for Christmas."

They advanced shyly, but they came, and every face glowed with sudden, eager hope. Joy Filler, Angela's little sister, broke the silence. "You for Christmas is best," she piped. "Next, me'd like popcorn. I've never had any."

"You for Christmas." It was absolute sincerity. Popcorn!

Millicent felt tears close to the surface, and she hugged little Joy. That eased the situation, and in a moment she was hearing ardent wishes intermingled with the small news that spiced her daily routine. Kitty Holder furnished the climax. "Simon Twill's has named their baby 'Millicent'," she announced, "and they would have used your middle name if they knew what it was. They want to 'member you by her."

That night Millicent curled under Mrs. Eli's best quilts and let go the tears she had held back all that harrowing day. She had made inquiries after school, and had had every hope completely squelched. There was no way by which she could escape a Christmas at Angel Cove and it seemed to her the most cruel thing that had ever entered her life.

After her first flood of grief, she let her mind go back over every detail of her coming to the place, teacher for the new school, an innovation at the Cove. It had seemed a grand adventure then. She had come by boat, stopping at many out-ports where flowers spangled the hills and the greenery came down to meet the water. She had liked her first view of the Cove. The bare rocks looked as if they had been scalped of sod, yet there was a grandeur to the whole that awed her, held her. The small homes nestled here and there where cellars were possible, the store and school looking important, and a fringe of rock be-yond that a sculptor might have chiselled from the grey stone.

The people had been very nice. She had met most of them at a pie social and then had been invited to many homes. She liked Peleg Filler and his wife. She had had supper many times with Bride and Abel Harmon. She enjoyed Aunt Mary Pertwee and her humble husband, Pete. They were wonderful people, all of them, even Amos Boone and his huge wife, Hannah Belle.

There had been a warm welcome. Enthused by it, she had pictured Eli as a sea-worn Viking, and Mrs. Eli as serving a nameless martyrdom for her daily bread. Little Mary was her slave from the first day, and from every child she gained the same response. The late summer days had passed gloriously. Every week had something new, something of variety for her, but then autumn had chilled her enthusiasm. Bit by bit, there had crept into her existence a longing to see her home again, and at last, in full bitterness, she had faced homesickness.

But she had finished the fall term. The three trustees would have been dismayed if she had hinted at any other course. Peleg Filler, tall, bony, and matter-of-fact, she avoided. He was too awk-ward in her presence. Abel Harmon, polite and good-natured, was the trustee she relied on. She knew he was guided largely by his wife, and he had also become the village fiddler. The teasing, foot-tapping music of his violin was the chief delight of Saturday nights when little parties were held. Like the others, Abel held book-learning in deep, uneasy respect, but he was intuitive to a comforting degree and acted as a pilot when Millicent seemed likely to encounter stormy weather. Joram Holder, third of the trustee trio, was aged, and whiskered warmly. It was legend that when he trimmed his beard it was a sign that spring had come, and Millicent now thought that spring was years away.

She turned uneasily in her bed as she heard timbers snapping with frost. Two weeks until Christmas, and another week till New Year's. Then a long journey by dog team, which she dreaded. What horrible luck! She resolved fiercely she would tell Abel they must pay her board during the extra three weeks, and with the thought, she fell asleep.

There was no rapping on the stovepipe in the morning, and when Millicent woke she heard Mrs. Eli moving, soft-footed, about her work, and hushing Mary to whispers.

It was terribly cold and there was an icy glitter to everything outside. Mrs. Eli bustled about, getting the breakfast she had prepared and kept warm in the oven. She greeted Millicent cheerfully. "Mrs. Peter Holder sent word over she'd like you for company a few days," she said. "And the others'd be proud to have you visit 'round."

Visit 'round! Millicent shuddered. But when she had eaten, she could not endure longer Eli's booming voice, the sight of his big hairy hands and bony wrists, disfigured by sea boils.

Nets! Gear! Was there anything else in the world beyond cod and herring and caplin, and tides and boats and trawl? At the beginning she had liked to hear so much talk about "fish goin'" and cod traps, and the staccato humming of motorboats, daily, was music that enlivened the Cove. But fall had brought the northeasters. Day after day they had blown, cold, wet, foggy, dying and rousing a dozen times until they had worn her courage thin, and she had figured into days, even into meals at Eli's table, her time of service.

"I'll go to Mrs. Peter's," she said suddenly, and went, leaving little Mary wistful.

Mrs. Peter was another "until death do us part" sort of wife, and her gladness at having the teacher call was so apparent that it brought a blush to Millicent's cheeks. The house was nearer the sea than Eli's and there seemed stronger odours of cod and rope and sea boots, but Peter's violin made her forget them. He played low, crooning melodies that made Millicent feel that she was in the midst of some deep peculiar dream from which she would awaken and find herself at home. Then he switched to quicker, sharper notes, reminding her of days when the wind shrilled mockingly and there was not a gull on wing. It seemed impossible that he could be but another of the Cove men, with sea sores on his wrists and his face a colour like preservation varnish.

"I like that playin'," Mrs. Peter murmured to Millicent. "He enjoys himself with that, and when we're alone he plays pieces just for me, all slidin' notes and pickin'. It's real sweet."

Millicent was startled. She had not thought to find such things at Angel Cove, and a lump came to her throat, then a burning desire to be home engulfed her. She knew the music had caused it, and she could not speak. Peter and his wife seemed to understand. They sat by the stove and said little.

Evening brought one of the Holders of the Cove. There were so many, Millicent was never sure of their identity, but this one had a grin that looked as much a part of his apparel as his trousers. "Us want to bring Granny over," he said. "We've had her a month, and we're havin' my boy, Joe, and his lot in for Christmas."

He was wearing a red sweater, a shade that made Millicent think of descriptions she had read of bullfighting, and he talked pleasantly as if winter were ideal weather.

When he had gone, Millicent turned to Mrs. Peter. "Is Granny relation to you?" she asked. It seemed to her a heartless thing to move the old lady at such a time.

"No," said Mrs. Peter. "Her has no relations."

"No relations!" Millicent could not understand. Granny was one of the Cove treasures, a wrinkled little old lady with the kindest blue eyes, held to her chair by rheumatism and vague with reverie, but always cheerful.

"No, her has none. Her had five boys. Two were lost on the ice, one at the herrin' boats, one died of flu, and the last were crushed workin' down along at the pulp mill. Her is kept by movin' around the place."

"Kept by movin' around." A village charge, dependent on charity, moved as accommodations were needed! Millicent's eyes welled full with pity.

Granny was transferred by sled the next day, swathed in blankets, helpless as a child, and when she was seated in Peter's kitchen, she was delighted at the sight of Millicent.

"So glad you're stayin', dearie," she said, "for it'll be more of a Christmas with you here."

More of a Christmas! When she had grasped fully Granny's meaning, Millicent knew why little Mary had watched her so hungrily, had been so often hushed by Mrs. Eli. Christmas, at the Cove, was often lacking cheer, but Christmas with the teacher to transform things was another matter. Listening to Granny, Millicent thought of a number of small toys in her trunk, novelties selected before leaving St. John's. She had had an indefinite idea of using them to appease a kindergarten class, and there had been none. As soon as she got back to Eli's tomorrow, she would get them out and wrap them.

Granny rambled on. She talked of hard years, lean years, of "scrabbling along" when credit at the store was only for "dry flour," and blueberries were a summer manna, and Millicent saw the Cove fold in a different light. They were heroic, splendid. They made her think of her father and mother.

"I've been makin' a 'membrance for you," Granny said shyly. "It's an 'art' and I hope you like it."

An "art"! Millicent had wanted to protest a gift, but the warmth in Granny's blue eyes held her dumb. An "art"? She did not know, could not think what an "art" was.

Two of the bigger boys got a Christmas tree for the school. It was a scraggly spruce, but Millicent guessed how far they had gone over the barrens to get it, and told them it exceeded all her expectations. Every child was eager to help with the decorations and a huge star was placed above the tree, a greeting banner strung across the room. Millicent surveyed it. "Merry Christmas to you." She was almost overwhelmed. It was so easy to cry, so hard not to. She worked hard purposely, so that she would fall asleep without thinking when she went to bed.

The scholars made a huge, red paper bell, and it shouted of other bells, real bells, church bells pealing Christmas gladness at home, sleigh bells jingling in the streets, shop windows ablaze with lights, wreaths of holly, gay friends, home. In a week, she had dammed back a year's hysteria.

Peter was a grand help. He fixed the tree on an upturned trawl tub. "It's wonderful," he said, "all this. Us never had a tree at our house." Then he looked at Millicent curiously. "You're never stiff-necked here," he said. "Do you like it?"

"Why, yes," said Millicent bravely. "It's," she used his own word, "wonderful."

He looked at her closely, and smiled. "Us thought you would like better to be home," he said.

Millicent could hardly wait until he had gone. She had to shed some tears. Home! Her mother waiting, inquiring about the boats. All the ribboned gifts ready, the house decorated, the phone ringing. "Has Milly got home yet? Gee, isn't she coming?"

She went back to Eli's and went to bed early, scarcely speaking with Mrs. Eli. Never in her life had she been so miserable, and when she finally slept she dreamed that grizzled harbour seals with beards were poking their heads through the Cove ice and booming a mocking "Merry Christmas." Then she was shaken. "Quick! Come out! The house is afire."

It was Mrs. Eli tugging at her, pulling her to the floor, flinging a blanket around her, leading her to the stairs. Acrid, blinding smoke engulfed them. There were frantic calls outside, much shouting, excited voices.

Millicent was glad she had her bed socks on. The cold was as keen as a fish knife and she had scant time to escape. Outside, little Mary, white-faced and silent, was in the path, and Mrs. Eli came carrying bedding into the snowdrift. Bewildered, shaking with cold, Millicent watched men rush into the house with tubloads of snow.

"Ugh! Oooooh!" She was gasping with cold as she struggled to get from the deeper snow. There were more shouts, and Eli came into the drifts carrying Millicent's trunk. She wondered how he had gotten through the smoke. Then someone seized her as if she were a child, picked her up, and carried her to Peter's house. It was a grand relief to be so taken and she almost snuggled in the strong arms, feeling sure it was Peter who held her.

Mrs. Peter was putting a kettle on the stove as Millicent was lowered to the floor beside her. Little Mary had just raced in. Millicent turned to thank her carrier—and was dumbfounded to face not Peter but another Holder, one with bulging red features. "You'll be all right here," he said awkwardly, and was gone.

"Oh—oh, I—" was all Millicent managed.

"They've got it out." Mrs. Peter's cry was reverently thankful as she turned from watching Eli's house. "I've made up a bed for you," she went on. "You stay here. Things'll be all upset over there for a day or so anyhow."

Millicent did not care where she stayed. She wondered what else could happen to her. Then she heard voices in the kitchen. Mrs. Eli was there, and Millicent gleaned that she was indirectly the cause of the fire. Mrs. Eli had been keeping "extry heat" to make it warm enough for the teacher, and had dozed as she sat in her chair by the stove. The pipe had overheated.

Knowing how much work Mrs. Eli did in a day, Millicent sobbed softly. She was sorry she had caused so much trouble, and then, unnerved, she sobbed again, sorry for herself. She wanted only one thing, to get back home, and then she would never trouble the Cove people again. She wondered if her mother was listening to beautiful Christmas music, there beside the radio, and steam heat, and comfort. She cried herself to sleep. Fortunately, the fire did little damage. Mrs. Eli scrubbed and cleaned all day, and the next night Millicent slept in her own bed again.

Three days passed like ages, days not lived but endured, then it was Christmas Eve. Millicent made pans of molasses candy. She had to do something to ease her tense nerves. There would be eight days more, then the dog team. She had begun counting the hours.

It was impossible to sleep when she got in bed. There had been a final placing of gifts, and she was glad that she had with her a ring she had not shown anyone. It was too small for her finger, so she had put it on the tree for Granny. She had bought pipes at the company store for Peter and Eli, and a knife for Abel Harmon. Then she had prepared a packet for Mrs. Eli, a bluestone brooch that her mother had given her on her birthday. But all thoughts of the morrow slipped away and her homesickness surged back. Angel Cove seemed isolated from the rest of the world. Never had she been so wretchedly miserable.

"Merry Christmas, teacher!" Millicent woke and stared at little Mary, who had been permitted the privilege of waking her.

"And—and to you, Mary." Millicent struggled with the words. She had wakened heartsick.

"You not well, teacher?"

"Yes, sure I'm well, Mary. Tell Mother I'll be right down for breakfast." Millicent forced a smile.

In the kitchen, Mrs. Eli eyed her shrewdly as she went down. Eli was as eager as a boy to get to the schoolhouse. "Are you homesick, dearie?" Mrs. Eli had come to Millicent's chair and had put an arm around her.

"No," said Millicent tremulously. "Not—not much."

On her way to the school, she saw two men moving Granny on a sled and realized they were taking her to the school. Inside, the building was crowded. Eli and his wife and little Mary were together, and Peter joined his wife and family. There seemed to be Holders everywhere. Families, parents, and children, eager, happy families, homes....

"Angela Holder," called Millicent, taking down the first package. It was a doll that could roll its eyes, and Angela shrieked with delight. Mrs. Eli was radiant as she fondled her brooch. Eli put his pipe in his mouth and would not remove it. Peter was jubilant when he unwrapped a fine pocket knife.

Millicent could hardly restrain her emotions as she undid little gifts for herself, trifles that had meant much effort or hard-earned money. Then Granny got her ring. "It's the first I've ever had," quavered the old lady, tears of joy in her blue eyes. "I were married by a borried one and there was never enough to spare to buy one. Nobody'll ever take that off my finger. Bless you, Miss Millicent."

Last of all, Millicent found the "art" from Granny. It was a soft, limp object, and she unwrapped it carefully. It was a hooked motto, red and grey and blue, simple enough, yet with every thread pulled with loving care by Granny's partly crippled hands.

"I got the red out of an old sweater," said Granny, "and the grey were a muffler. I hope you like it. It seemed natural I'd do them words."

Natural! Millicent was glad the thronging excited ones hid her for a moment. She was gripped with hysteria. Then she seemed stifled by a million different emotions. She fought them and found a strange calm. It was as if she saw on a screen a portrait of herself and Granny. Granny, lone, old, helpless, homeless, buffeted by uncounted years, and smiling and producing her "art" as if it were "natural."

Then she saw herself. Five months from home and bemoaning the loss of three weeks. Three weeks! And Granny! Why, why....

Millicent sprang up and joined in the fun. Games were starting. She kissed little Mary, almost sticking to molasses candy. Then she threw a challenging forfeit at Eli and laughed gaily at the bewilderment on his lean face. In a moment he was in pursuit, and Angel Cove rocked in merriment. It was the merriest Christmas they could imagine. And Millicent had a wonderful Christmas dinner of lovely baked cod, and salmon, and fig pudding.

Granny's motto was placed so that all could see it. Its three words were "Home, Sweet Home."

Lingering Melodies

Wayne Curtis

Wayne Curtis weaves a bittersweet tale set in 1950s Miramichi, featuring the old-time traditions of celebrating Christmas in a one-room schoolhouse in rural New Brunswick.

"I will sing one song for my old Kentucky home." We had stood beside our school desks and sung each Friday afternoon, holding a copy of *The Silver Book of Songs*, an anthology of verse and melodies that included "Swanee River," "O Canada," "The Maple Leaf Forever," and "God Save the Queen." These songs mixed nicely with our dreams of the future, ambitions bigger than life. There had been American influence, yes even then, in the songs and the radio programs. *The Lone Ranger and Tonto* had been in the schoolyard during lunch hour, and there was a teepee made of poles on the riverbank out back. Inside the classroom a kind of discipline prevailed, and there was great tension in our focus on learning. And sometimes, even now, when I hear those old songs, the symbols in them bring back my struggles with long division, the War of Independence, the poetry of Wilfred Campbell. Old school and old home, in the days when my father was still my hero and our little community was the most important place on earth to live.

I think of this now as I walk in my father's fields, just as I used to do almost fifty years ago. I am gathering the limbs from an apple tree corpse to burn in the old fireplace. I have come home from Toronto, where I play second violin for the Toronto Symphony Orchestra. My sister, Sara, will arrive from Halifax later today and we will spend Christmas here with the folks. Sara, now a film producer in that city, works very hard. I am sure she will be played out from the drive here, but it will be a nice change of pace for us both. We will have a chance to reminisce; no doubt we will talk on into the night, as we do at such times. Again we will try to fathom it all, look to an ever-shortening future and try to put our past into perspective, how we got to where we are. During such talks, I generally have trouble. Because of what time does to memories, it is always hard for me to see my youth clearly. Sometimes Sara will have to set me straight.

However, one part I do remember well is the school I attended for eight years, before I went into grade nine, before the buses came and took us to the big regional academy in the city. This, and a teacher whose name was Catherine Green, a young woman who influenced my life. I think of her now as I approach the old school grounds.

As an adolescent, I had hated school. I would sit inside the schoolhouse door and listen to freedom: blue jays crying in hawthorn trees, crickets singing in the playground wildflowers, vagabond winds rattling against a slanting flagstaff. When I hunted partridge in the black alder swamps, where

I would steal away whenever possible, the wind carried the sweet incense of autumn: the smoke of bonfires, the lure of river and woods, the crack of deer rifles, the smell of decaying leaves under my rubbers. Even now, a series of images repeat themselves inside me, each from a different person, a different place, and of course a different state of mind. They live on in the old school songs and poetry like coals in the ashes of burnt- out fantasies.

Along the line of smoky hills / the crimson forest stands...

"Indian Summer," a poem by Wilfred Campbell. I remember reciting this, standing by my school desk, glancing out the window to watch the early winter come down, wishing I were somewhere else. By the end of October, our clocks had been set back and darkness came early. The autumn rains slanted across bleached fields already frozen, the brooks and the river also frozen over. Then came the snow. At first only a little, like salt. Tiny pellets lay in dead leaves and on trays of ice along the roadway as my sister and I walked to school. It dusted about with the wind from passing vehicles and mixed with blowing sand to look like ashes. In the woods behind the school, snow zigzagged among trees to catch and hold on boughs and leave bare patches of frozen moss. It turned our cardboard teepee into porcelain, froze our boot tracks into china saucers. But this inspired a new exuberance in us because, by the end of November, Miss Green had started rehearsing her Christmas program, which we regarded as a break from schoolwork.

At home I had put in my order to Santa for a new jack-knife, but this gift was uncertain. Our parents spoke of the hardships of past winters. They cautioned us children that it would be cruel to expect much, because times were bad. So, as the Christmas season approached, windbreaks and snow fences were erected, our house banked and shuttered. Our dreams we adjusted many times, selfish wants relinquished to dire needs, to optional practicalities (if things went right); and these simple necessities were to be shared equally by brothers and sisters.

This was the time in our lives when Christmas brought a lot of magic. Everything that we had encountered since Halloween would have been a part of the Yuletide season. The woods suddenly became scattered with little red berries and pine buds; the trees had taken on a new shade of silver, a stronger scent of balsam; and the frozen river had become a place to test our hand-me-down skates. Even the old schoolhouse and our teacher, Miss Green, grasped the spirit.

My mother and Sara, who was in grade four, sat by the piano in the living room and sang "O Christmas Tree," a song which my sister had been rehearsing for the school concert. Our mother was "not well" that year and would not be coming to the program. She would have a new baby in February.

Our school was a one-room clapboard building with a porch, three long windows down the side, a black weathered woodshed, and two backhouses (Girls and Boys), which stood among hawthorn trees at the edge of the playground. The schoolhouse was heated by a sowbellied wood stove with the words "Enterprise Foundries—Sackville New Brunswick," cast in the shape of a horseshoe on the door.

Miss Green, a tall, willowy, and delicate-looking blond, appeared quite stiff, and she seldom smiled. Her big, brown eyes were easily made tearful—I am guilty of having made her cry—and during study periods she sighed a lot. She was in her early twenties (although she seemed much older to us then), convent educated, and teaching here on a local license. She was paying for room and board at the old McLaren Farm next to ours. She had come from the southern part of the province, a brooding townswoman who had not been accepted in our community. There was mystery about her past, and a lot of gossip.

"She plays that long-haired stuff on the fiddle. It's certainly not the kind of music that anyone around here can stand," I heard Mrs. Crumb once say in my father's store. "Or 'violin,' as she calls it."

"I never could see where she was all that good-looking, either," Mr. Porter added and winked at my father as he spit tobacco juice into a tin can.

Because I was big for my age, I stood awkwardly among the smaller children. We sang the school songs and recited allegiance to our flag, which was held by two clothespins on a string. Some days there were only seven or eight of us in school. I was in charge of tending fires, so I had to be there early. I also carried water from a brook under the hill and kept the doorstep shovelled, as well as a pathway to the outhouses and woodshed. For these chores. I received free violin lessons from Miss Green one night a week at her boarding house. Everyone else my age was working in the woods.

At school, Miss Green was very strict. We were not allowed to whisper or smile or glance out the windows. If she caught us at any of these things, she stood us facing into the corner for a long time. Sometimes we got the strap, which she kept in her desk drawer beneath a rainbow chocolate box containing pencils, erasers, paper clips, and elastic bands. Miss Green appeared to be cold all the time and sat with her feet up on the stove. Occasionally she would ask me to go to the shed for firewood. Once I spilled an armload of kindling, pretending to trip and fall as I came through the door. Chunks scattered into the aisles. The other kids laughed. Miss Green looked at me with great disgust. Yet I had done this, not to provoke the teacher, but as a respite against the relentless afternoon. As I gathered up the sticks, embarrassed, I realized my stunt was not funny.

On a sunless day in late November, all day Miss Green sat, staring off into space, with her coat on and her feet up on the stove. The next day she was ill, and there was no school. She was laid up for almost two weeks. It was rumoured at the local store that she was expecting. Some said she already had a baby, whom she gave away. Others said her baby was born dead and was burned in the big stove at the foot of the McLaren's stairs. That, or it had been buried under the doorstep. Of course, there was no baby.

When Miss Green was back in school, the gossip turned to excessive discipline, because she kept some of us late to work out long division when we were needed at home to do our evening chores. But by then we were well into rehearsing recitations, songs, and dialogues for the Christmas program. The girls had drawn little holly leaves and berries around the edge of the blackboard with coloured chalk. Crayoned drawings hung in windows. The school had been thoroughly scrubbed and smelled of disinfectant and new stove polish. Because I was the biggest, I had been sent to the swamp for a Christmas tree, a tree which, according to the class, was too tall and open. Miss Green said I should have gone to more open woods, where a tree would have room to reach out. But we decorated this tree with haws, rosehip berries, strings of frozen cranberries we had gathered from the swamp, and our gifts for the teacher. I did not have a present for Miss Green, so I wrapped the wool mittens my mother had knit for me and put them on the tree. I later told my mother I had lost them. Before the program, our school was filled with magic. I carried chairs from around the community, filling the aisles and the back of the classroom. During lunch, our teacher had gone home and put on a new black dress, red sweater, and long beads. She looked very nice, but even in that dress there was a sternness about her that kept us all on our guard. She had also brought her violin case, which she stood in the corner. She intended to play a Christmas number for the parents.

There was a light wind, and it was snowing softly as we sat and waited for members of the community. Miss Catherine Green paced the floor. Her delicate fingers played with her beads in a kind of prayer. She stopped only to look, preoccupied, out the window, past the crayoned Santas into the fading light and the stretch of road that led to the schoolhouse. She often stared that way, like she couldn't see the obvious. I had come to regard her with a feeling of defensiveness, as if I had secretly taken her side in things. I could feel that she had sensed this in me, because she often spared me the hard questions. A bond grew, ever so fragile, like an antique Christmas decoration.

The afternoon was hurrying past to defy us all. And no one was coming. At quarter to three, Miss Green decided to go ahead with the program. I struggled within my adolescent timidity amid giggles, as I recited in front of the class, who had heard it a hundred times, and a dozen empty chairs:

Away up in the rocky north
Where Christmas trees won't grow
All snug and cozy in his bed
Lives a little Eskimo.
His tiny stockings and mukluks
He hangs up by the fire.
He lives so close to Santa Claus
The reindeer never tire.

I took a bow and sat down. There was applause—not for me, but for the liberty of making a noise here. The five schoolgirls, my sister Sara among them, stood in a row at the front of the room and sang, "Santa Claus is coming, we will welcome him with glee, we'll hang a gift for everyone upon our Christmas tree...hurrah, hurrah." With each "hurrah" their hands made a sweeping gesture as if to grab something invisible. They bowed together and went to their seats. Then I went outside and stood in the cold entryway. On cue, I knocked and came in, a beggar in search of a remedy for my aching back. I rolled on the schoolhouse floor, moaning and gasping. Pockets of laughter broke out. Even our teacher, who seemed to have no time for folly, offered a piteous half-smile. As I gathered the chairs after the program, Miss Green, sitting at her desk, took a handkerchief from her sleeve. She wiped her nose and dabbed her soft brown eyes.

"Christmastime," she sobbed, "I thought some of the parents just might come...."

The next day, snow puffed off roofs and drifted into dooryards to make cliffs in the lee of buildings. Flowerpots that sat on open verandas became tubs of ice cream. Fence posts became frosted Popsicles, and our field's shaggy spruce grew into giant silver bells, as we gathered the dead limbs of apple trees and carried them home for the hearth fire. Our parents made much ado about Santa coming down the chimney and keeping his suit clean of the black ash. I can still remember the restless night that followed: the turkey, the church service, the visits from neighbours.

Then suddenly, amid all the singing, fairy tales, storm fear, and hearth fires, as though the whole event had been executed by the hands of a magician, Christmas came and went, almost without us seeing it happen. It was like reality had gobbled up our pre-Christmas illusions—everything we had looked forward to for months was over in a matter of hours. Cap guns and plastic-faced cotton dolls with tilting blue eyes, the red fire engines and twisted candy canes, lay scattered in a haze of tinselled rejections, selfish desire, and false hopes. Disillusioned with ourselves, with each other, and with our parents, we were left trying to adjust back into the harsh world of winter. In January, we pondered the obscure poems of Sir Charles G. D. Roberts and Robert Frost. Whose woods these are, I think I know. Frost's "Stopping by Woods on a Snowy Evening" is still a favourite.

One afternoon, while working out our long division on the blackboard, Miss Green confronted me about carving my initials in a heart next to hers on the door of the girls' outhouse. She said she had seen it during lunch hour and recognized my printing. She knew about the pocket knife I had received for Christmas.

"My brother William did it when he was home from the woods for the holidays!" I pleaded to her, stone-faced in front of the class.

"Don't you lie to me, Scott Millen!" she yelled, and tugged my sleeve to march me into the porch so the others couldn't see. The blistering strap fell upon my hands, and Miss Green's eyes filled with tears. It was like she was being punished for her indifference, or that she needed to vent her grievance with the community against one of us. I grabbed the strap, threw it on the floor, and ran for home. I think now that I did this to help spare her the moment. I knew I had pushed her to wield the strap, and I was sorry. In the evening, my mother made me go to the teacher's boarding house to apologize to Miss Green for carving the initials, lying about it, and running away. I can remember standing nervously in the McLarens' parlour, my cap in my hands.

"Miss Green, I'm so sorry about what happened there today in school," I said. "It was a terrible thing I did."

At this she smiled and squeezed my arm. She said that neither of us should ever mention the incident again.

Toward spring, my mother invited Miss Green to our house for supper. It was a sunny evening when she walked up the highway from her boarding house; the wind caught her scarf and the skirts of her long brown coat as she proudly carried her violin case. She sat in the kitchen rocker and talked to my mother in her refined schoolteacher's voice. We ate in the dining room that night, and everyone was polite. After the meal, my mother asked her to play.

Miss Catherine Green stood in the centre of the parlour with sheet music on a stand and tapped her foot up and down. Her long hair shone beneath the electric lights as she played. She handled the polished instrument so delicately, holding it to her chin as though it was a part of her soul while she played with four quick, lithe fingers. Everyone in our house could see that Miss Green had a lot of class. She performed the kind of music that none of us except my mother (who could play by ear) really understood or appreciated. Until then, we had heard it only on the radio. She played the theme from the radio show *The Lone Ranger*—William Tell's "Overture in B-flat"—and "Tara's Theme," which I didn't know at the time was from the motion picture *Gone With the Wind*. Miss Green's music filled the room with images well beyond the physical and metaphoric borders of our small community. She seemed pleased when we applauded, blushing openly as she put her instrument back in its case. I knew then I wanted to learn to play that kind of music. My new fantasy was more real than any of the others. I worked hard at my music after that night.

In March, Miss Green was sick again, and for a time Mr. McLaren drove her to school in his old square-top car. Then the school was closed, and a letter was sent to homes saying that the teacher was suffering from tuberculosis and the doctor was admitting her to the sanatorium in Saint John. No grades were given at our school that year.

From her bed at the sanatorium, Catherine Green exchanged letters with my mother. Once she sent a black-and-white photo of herself propped up with pillows against her runged bedstead. She always asked how I was doing in school and if I was keeping up with my music. Sometime later, she wrote to say that she was getting married to a young doctor. We never heard from Catherine Green again. I think of her now as I walk through the old orchard to what used to be our open fields. The ground is damp and brown. Dark clouds appear to be holding up the snow. It seems like every practical thing from those days has fallen down and blown away. The stems of ragged cattails have buckled, the rosehip and the hawthorn have withered and decayed, and a new growth of shrub has infested my father's farm. Where the schoolhouse once stood there is now only a clearing, the abandoned sheds having burned, the classroom moved for use as a machine shed by a neighbour. Only the girls' outhouse remains. It stands on the site, slanting and forlorn. I walk over and check its door, but the scars of my youth have long since grown over. I think of Catherine Green, and I try to grasp some of the spirit of that faded day, when a pretty blond woman played the violin for my family. The memory dances like a distorted video, but brightens now with a drifting flake of snow, and the lingering melody of an old school song.

Margaret's Masterpiece

David Weale

This marvelous story from An Island Christmas Reader *portrays the painstaking efforts that the women of Prince Edward Island were prepared to undertake to achieve the perfect Christmas for their friends and family.*

The wallpaper on her bedroom wall had one of those repetitive floral patterns where each constellation of blossoms was the same as every other, and where each connected to the next in exactly the same way. The only place it was different was in the corner, where the last piece had been cut to make it fit. The paper had been her own choice, but sometimes she would lie on her bed and squint, vainly attempting to locate one pattern that was in any way different from the rest.

Margaret had a husband, a house, and five children who depended on her. There wasn't much money, but she was able to make ends meet, and, as far as she knew, there wasn't anyone who had anything bad to say about her, except for one woman up the road who had something bad to say about everyone. She knew every single person in her district by name, as well as their politics, their religion, and who their people had been; and everyone knew her in the same way. There was comfort and security in that knowing; yet for all of that, sometimes her own life seemed blurred—unremarkable and unnoted. It wasn't anything she could explain to anyone, or even to herself, but she felt it most days. It might have been easier somehow if there had been some great disappointment in her life, or if she had been able to spend her time nursing the regret of secret dreams unfulfilled. But it wasn't like that. The regret had no name, and the discontent no particular shape.

Sometimes it occurred to her how much she was like her mother. That wasn't altogether unpleasant, but she always felt stirrings of annoyance when Ruth, her aunt, would call her by her mother's name. It was the same feeling she had when her husband would call her "Mom;" or when, shortly after her marriage, she received a letter in the mail addressed to "Mrs. John McIsaac," and stared at it for a moment, wondering who it was for.

But Margaret seldom gave way to her feelings. Like everyone around her she was, most of the time, a careful person, measuring out her emotions in pinches and teaspoonful, according to the recipe of inherited wisdom. She had learned early that you had to watch every penny, and every word, and that impulsive or extravagant behaviour of any kind was the best way of inviting criticism. Once, early in her marriage, she had sent away in the Eaton's catalogue for a set of ruffled white curtains for the dining room window, and was chastised by her mother-in-law. "Well, Margaret," she said with affected nonchalance, "I'm surprised you've spent your money this way.

There might be a day coming when you'll wish you had it for something else, something you really need." She paused for just a moment and then added, "I'm sure the would look lovely, but the ones that are there would be considered perfectly fine by most." It stung, and after that Margaret kept the curtains hidden away in a bureau drawer.

Margaret's house, like her own life, was tidy and neat, but largely unadorned by anything which might be considered profusive or showy. The virtue of constraint was reinforced habitually, and eventually manifested itself in all her ways. But there was one notable exception to all of this. Margaret discovered that there was one day of the year when it was possible, without reprimand, to cast aside the everyday strictures of prudence, and to let loose in an outpouring of unstinting excess. That day was Christmas Eve.

The preparation began in the fall. She'd get her fruitcakes done before the end of October, wrap them in white cotton, and put them in a cake tin with some slices of apple to keep them moist. Then she'd put them in the cellar, in the wall, where her husband had cut out a special niche. As adults, her children could still remember going down to the cellar and opening the lid just to smell the cakes, and to anticipate the feast which, they knew, was already taking shape in their mother's mind.

As Christmas approached, her pantry shelves would begin to fill up with all the ingredients she would need: extra sugar and flour, raisins, dates, currants, cinnamon, suet and all the rest. Then, the day before Christmas Eve, she'd get her rabbits. The skinning and gutting took place in the barn, and it always amazed her children how she could perform the task with so little mess. One of them would hold the leg while she took a razor blade and made one neat stroke down the belly so that everything would fall out in one piece. One of her sons remembered that his arm would get sore, the way it would when he held the skein of yarn, but that his mother would make the time pass quickly by telling stories about when she was a girl and had to do the same thing.

About four o'clock on Christmas Eve she'd begin to panic. There was so much left to do. She'd instruct the children to get out all her good dishes, clean them, and set them on the big table, which she had covered with the white Christmas table-cloth with roses hand-stitched in the corner. Both leaves of the table were up, providing a large enough space for all the food, which would make an appearance before midnight. While all this was happening she'd be making her pies—lemon, apple, and raisin. All the old men loved raisin.

One year her oldest daughter, in an attempt to be help-ful, proceeded to cut the pies shortly after they had come out of the oven. Her mother intervened sharply. "Not now! Not now!" she scolded. The girl did not understand that her moth-er's Christmas Eve event was more than a meal. It was a pag-eant, and cutting the pies before the company arrived did not fit the script.

The children were sent to bed around nine o'clock, to be called in time for midnight Mass. When they were out of the way she'd set up the four or five card tables with chairs and centrepieces, then return to the stove for the final preparations. In just a few hours, it would all come together according to her carefully premeditated plan. By the time the children were roused for their trip to the church, the house was filled with the scent of cloves emanating from the pan of rabbit broth on the top of the stove. More than anything else it was that smell which announced the arrival of the great event.

Margaret didn't go to church. Her Christmas duty was right there, in the kitchen. Her husband accompanied the children, and it was his responsibility to make sure all the guests were invited home after the service. By the time they got back everything was out. The table was full. There was rabbit pie; creamy, golden mustard-pickles and chow; squares of cheese; slices of homemade bread an inch thick; the cakes from the cellar, now out of their tins and sliced and arranged decorously on special plates; a dish of divinity fudge; and the pies at the back, side by side, the droplets on the top of the lemon meringue catching the light like tiny Christmas ornaments.

When everyone came in, she'd be standing by the stove, putting on the tea, looking like she was ready to burst. The guests, in an elevated state of Christmas goodwill, would remark how wonderful everything looked, and year after year she'd say it was nothing, a comment which belied the obvious aura of achievement and consummation that radiated from her. Someone would say, "Margaret, you're a marvel!" and she would say, "Go on now!" and tell them to help them themselves.

She never sat down during the entire meal, not for a minute, just circulated continuously, replenishing the plates and teacups. "Would you like some more?" she would ask rhetorically, as she deposited a second or third piece of rabbit pie on the half-empty plate. "Margaret, I couldn't eat another bite!" someone would protest, but if there was even the slightest hint of hesitation, she would proceed undeterred. "Oh! Have some more," she would say. "All we get in this life is a bite to eat."

From one year's end to the next there was nothing in Margaret's experience to match the way she felt during the brief time when her family and friends were at their places, enjoying her creation. She moved among the tables with such flourish and aplomb that it seemed the entire meal might well have been scripted and choreographed. For those few moments, Margaret was in her glory, vividly and triumphantly herself. It was a grand achievement, flawlessly performed and universally acclaimed within her small circle.

Late in the night, long after the last grateful guest had departed, and the children, taut with excitement, had finally dropped off to sleep, she finished cleaning up. It was time to fill the stocking, and to start thinking about the goose and the next day's meal, which always seemed to her an anticlimax. She was tired now, and the veins in her legs were aching. At three o'clock, she sat down in the rocking chair beside the stove with a cup of tea and a piece of bread. The house was quiet, and she felt a great serenity in herself as she savoured the events of the past few hours. She glanced over at the table, now bare except for the tablecloth. It would stay there for one more meal, and then go back into the drawer, beside the ruffled curtains.

This is Our Willie: A Christmas Story

Michael O. Nowlan

*Set in Millbank, on the Miramichi, is Michael
O. Nowlan's story of the extraordinary Willie
McMatthews, whose Christmas hand-carvings
were dismissed as junk—until a stranger came to
town.*

Willie McMatthews lived at Elm Grove, on the far
end of the Lower Millbank road. Even though he
was only a mile from the centre of the village, he
was considered to be far enough away. Since he
only came to Snow's Store once a week, early every Thursday
morning, the villagers felt quite safe. Although everyone was
afraid of Willie, no one could remember his having hurt a soul.

When Willie's mother died five years before, everyone
wondered what would become of "the quare fellow on the lower road," as Ruby O'Neil always called him. The gossip group at
Snow's Store was intent on having Willie "sent away to a home
where we would be rid of him." But Willie remained. In fact,

he refused to leave the old place, which had been named by his great-grandfather. To him, the "Grove" was a special spot he had to look after, and look after it he did. Many thought him strange or unbalanced, but Willie's place was meticulously kept.

Willie lived on a pension and an inheritance. Before his mother died, she set up a plan whereby he would receive a cheque each month. This he cashed at Snow's Store, where he had a credit account. Most of the things he used—food, clothing, tools—came from Snow's.

Although he was able to manage his affairs and keep a tidy home, Willie McMatthews was always an outcast to the Millbank society. At least, this was so until Christmas Eve a few years ago.

The major event in Millbank was the annual fall bazaar. Held in late November, it featured numerous handcrafted items which were in much demand as Christmas gifts. Actually, the Millbank bazaar was one of the most popular attractions in the region. People came from up and down the river to stock up for Christmas. There were jams, jellies, fruitcakes, plum puddings, mincemeat, and all types of fruits and vegetables. It was the handiwork displays, though, that received the greatest attention. Maud Wilsil led the way with her famous "Granny quilts," which always brought good prices from the upriver city people.

Unlike many bazaars, Millbank's was not sponsored by some club or organization. Like an old fashioned market, each displayer paid twenty dollars for a space to sell his goods. Since the profit people made was their own, many looked forward to a good sale to enhance their own Christmas spending.

Once its fame was well established, the Millbank Bazaar needed little advertising. A preview of some of the items could be seen from early October, because Lloyd Snow allocated one window as a display area. Each displayer was allowed to put one labelled item in the window.

One Thursday morning in late September, when Willie came in for his usual groceries, the pack he carried was bulging. Lloyd Snow thought this strange, because the pack was always empty when Willie arrived. By now, Lloyd knew most of the items Willie always bought, so he quickly got them together. He never wanted to have Willie "hang around too long because it was bad for business with that creep in the store."

This week, Willie added a small can of peaches and a package of peppermints to the collection. Since it was pay week, he took out his cheque and handed it to the storekeeper. When Lloyd gave back the change he had coming to him after the month's account was settled, Willie looked him in the eye. At the same time, he fussed with the buckle on his pack.

"I was wondering, Mista Snow, if you mightn' put ma carvin' in the display window."

"Now, Willie, what kind of carving do you have?" Willie was always whittling at something. That he could make excellent whistles out of alder wood was widely known. No one, however, paid much attention to most of the things Willie carved, because they were often crude and sometimes offensive.

"Let's see it, Willie," insisted the proprietor. He knew without seeing it that he would not put it on display, but he was curious. There was no way he would "ever clutter up his store window with any of the junk that Willie McMatthews carved." Lloyd Snow was a fierce and determined man and what he said was usually heeded in Millbank. There was no mayor, but often he served the same purpose. He had a dominating manner with which few argued.

Out of his pack, Willie drew a neat carving of a baby. Lloyd Snow almost gasped. It was a beautiful piece of work, and he knew Willie was thinking of Christmas and the crib.

"Have more," said Willie. "The Virgin, the Joseph—three of every each of them." Willie beamed. "Mista Snow, I have sheeps too and some angels. These for Christmas crib. Will you put to window?"

With that, Willie pointed toward the empty window space, which had already been cleared and prepared with fancy paper and streamers.

Lloyd Snow ran his finger over the smooth carving, and inwardly admired its fine quality, but there was no way he would display this "quare fellow's" work. What would everyone say? His pride would not let him do it.

Slowly, he shook his head. "Sorry, Willie; no one wants to buy that kind of thing at the Millbank bazaar. You can do your usual for us by setting up the tables and taking them down afterward. But make sure you stay out of the way and don't bother the customers. Now, you just take this back home."

"You—do not like what I do," Willie said hesitatingly. "This ma bes' work ever. I do it for Him." Willie pointed to the infant Lloyd was handing back.

"No, Willie. Now, let's forget the whole thing."

When bazaar day arrived, Millbank took on a festive atmosphere. Even though the old church hall was still used for the sale, many set up stalls outside, because it was bright and sunny and unusually warm for November.

By mid-afternoon, when much of the best material had been sold, Karl von Hauten, a Christmas tree buyer from New York who operated a business a few miles above Millbank, arrived in his white Cadillac. His arrival was important, because he always spent at least one hundred dollars on gifts "for the folks back in the States." The women, who knew his buying practices, scurried to boxes under tables to bring out items they kept hidden for the American buyer.

This year, however, von Hauten moved quickly through the sales area, looking at each display and frowning because he could not find what he wanted. He went up and down three times, buying only a pair of small mittens Mrs. Oldfellow offered him. As he turned to leave, he spotted Snow by the exit and asked if there were any of those handmade cribs that were on display last year.

"No," replied Lloyd. "Those were brought in by a fellow from Millerton. He only came once, and we haven't heard from him since. They were nice, though, and he sold them all."

"That's too bad," uttered the disgruntled tree buyer as he walked down the hall.

Willie, who was lurking in the shadows of the porch where he could not be seen, heard the conversation. Silently, he followed and caught up with him as he opened the door of his big car.

"Mista von Hauten, I make what you want at my place. Come an' I show you."

With a scowl, the tall American looked down at the decrepit creature in front of him. As he slammed the door of the Cadillac, he had a sudden inspiration. Maybe the old fool had something he could use. It wouldn't hurt to look.

By now, Willie was slouching back toward the hall with his shoulders bent lower then ever.

Von Hauten rolled down the window and called, "Willie!"

Willie stopped and looked around.

"It won't hurt me to look at what you have."

"I make figures to go in crib for Christmas. Make crib, too, if you like."

"Get in," said the American, and off they went to Elm Grove.

The next week at Snow's store, Willie used a fifty-dollar American bill to pay for his groceries. The following week, he had another. The story soon spread, but Willie would only say that Mr. von Hauten gave it to him. Only Snow suspected what had happened, and he dismissed it, thinking: "The guy must have been a fool to spend that much money on Willie's stuff."

The day before Christmas Eve, the Brunswick *Daily Times* had a special picture on the front page, with an attention-getting headline in large, bold letters: "FROM MILLBANK." The caption went on to say that the display of the traditional Christmas Crib in one of the largest department stores in New York City was carved by Willie McMatthews of Millbank. It also said there were three sets, all of which were owned by a Mr. von Hauten, a Christmas tree buyer from upstate New York.

Since the papers were delivered to Snow's Store, Lloyd was the first in Millbank to see the picture. He not only gasped this time; he almost fainted. "Our Willie," he breathed out loud. "How in tamation?"

That day, Christmas Eve, and for many months afterward, there was a newspaper clipping glued to a piece of red cardboard hanging in the door window of Snow's Store. Above it, in two-inch letters, were the words: "THIS IS OUR WILLIE."

Christmas Traditions

The Kneeling of the Cattle

Alden Nowlan

*With fondness and keen observation, Alden Nowlan
looks back on his early childhood years growing up
in rural, 1930s Nova Scotia, when the celebration
of the Christmas season with his family produced
some of his most heartwarming memories.*

At midnight on Christmas Eve, so my grandmother told me when I was a small boy, the cattle kneel in their stalls in adoration of the Christ Child, who was born in a stable.

When I got to be about eight years old, I asked her if she had ever seen them kneel. Of course not, she said. It was not a sight that God permitted human beings to see. She had heard of a man who hid in his barn, hoping to spy on the cattle. In punishment, God struck him blind.

She lived in Nova Scotia, but she might as easily have been an old peasant woman in Galicia or Moldavia.

Years later, I learned from a poem by Thomas Hardy that the legend of the kneeling cattle flourished among the peasantry of old, pre-industrial England. For all I know, it may have originated in the Middle Ages, or earlier.

The North Atlantic wind hurled itself against the house, roaring like a demented bear. The snow was piled in great Himalayan drifts between barn and house, so that there was a howling white valley between. Beyond the whiteness of the snow and the blackness of the night, the cattle sank to their knees in a barn warmed by the heat of their own bodies. There, to borrow a phrase from Robert Graves, is the iconotropic instant—the sacred picture—that best represents the Christmas of my earliest childhood.

We were poor. So poor that my memories of that poverty sometimes seem to me less private recollections than dark glimpses of the collective unconscious, dreams from another country and another century.

In 1933, the year I was born, my father worked in the lumber woods for fifty cents a day. Fifty cents a day! That sounds absurd, almost comical now—like something out of an Al Capp comic strip or *The Beverly Hillbillies* about the going wage in Pineapple Junction or Bugtussle. It wasn't funny then.

We were poor. And this was a poverty unlike that which afflicted the urban middle classes during the Depression. That kind of poverty compared with ours was a hit-and-run accident, in which the victim escapes death or serious injury, compared with a congenital and incurable disease.

Yet I can't remember a year when there wasn't a Christmas.

A year without a Christmas! That's been the subject of so many reminiscences. The child wakes up Christmas morning to find the expected miracle hasn't taken place; and his parents can only murmur lame excuses, laugh nervously and refuse to meet his eyes.

That never happened to me.

It's been said that hunger is the best spice. And it's been said that the good thing about hitting yourself on the head with a hammer is that it feels nice when you stop. About the only good thing about involuntary poverty is that, sometimes, it turns lead into gold.

If the three wise men had been wiser, they'd have known they needn't bring gold, frankincense, and myrrh to the Christ Child. He'd have been equally happy with a shiny button, a little sugared milk, and a single flower.

I can't recall that any new decorations were ever bought for our tree. There were two strands of crepe paper rope, one red and one green, a box of hollow coloured-glass balls, a tinsel star for the top, and some odds and ends of things. Every Christmas the ropes were a bit shorter, and there were one or two fewer glass balls. But there always seemed to be enough. Perhaps my father, seeing the supply of decorations had diminished, each year brought home a smaller tree than the year before. I doubt that, though, for the tree always reached from floor to ceiling.

If new decorations had appeared, I think we children would have been vastly pleased—but only at first, then we'd have begun to worry. It would have been a superstitious kind of worry. I think we'd have knocked on wood or performed some similar rite of exorcism if we'd been confronted with a third strand of paper rope, or another box of glass balls. For the old decorations weren't simply pretty things we hung on a tree: they were Christmas. We were even a little uncomfortable, just for an instant, if we happened to see them at any other time of year. To a small child, they looked so dead and yet so mystical thrown together in a heap in their cardboard box in a closet.

There were foods we ate only at Christmas, never at any other time. In retrospect, I suppose it was poverty that caused us to eat grapes, oranges, and nuts only at Christmas. But we didn't think of it that way at the time: we no more expected grapes in July than we expected snow. Those delicacies were sacramental to the season. At least, that's what children felt. It was as though Christ had ordained that they should be eaten in honour of his birth.

Naturally, we didn't put such thoughts into words; but I'm sure that's how we felt.

Consider the grapes. They were always red grapes, incidentally, never purple or green. The texture of those grapes was like a kiss. And they offered a trinity of tastes—the hot roughness of the skin; the cool secret inner pulp, so full of juice that you both drank and ate it; and the crisp, nutty seeds you broke between your teeth. Occasionally, when we were almost satiated, we separated skin, pulp, and seeds and ate them one after the other, so that the flavour of each was distinct. That was a religious rite, the eating of those grapes, although we didn't need to call it religious.

Oranges. We ate peeling and seeds as well as pulp, and it was like swallowing a piece of summer that had been rolled into a ball and preserved in honey. The pulp was as sweet as sunlight, the skin as acidulous as sunburn.

And nuts. The strange, almost sinister crab-shaped hearts of the walnuts, the meaty, slightly woody texture and taste of them. The white meat of the Brazil nuts that tasted like cake frosting. The rubbery, bittersweet hazel nuts. The protracted spiciness of the almonds. The peanuts, so salty and oily they tasted almost fishy. We opened them with a claw hammer on a piece of stove-wood, never having heard of nutcrackers.

There was ribbon candy, a corkscrew-shaped rainbow of colours and flavours: mint, banana, wintergreen, lemon, orange, cherry, and strawberry. Cinnamon sticks: tiny, cherry-pink walking sticks, the cinnamon encased in molasses candy. And barley toys, which we always ate last because they were shaped like little animals—elephants, tigers, horses, and camels—which we hesitated to destroy; and besides, they tasted like nothing except sugary water.

Dinner was chicken and roast pork. But after eating fruit, nuts, and candy all morning, we children were never very excited about dinner.

The gifts were mostly homemade, except for the occasional doll or box of crayons. Once there was a team of wooden horses, hand-carved with a jackknife and complete with harness and wagon. Another time a miniature ship, a tern schooner, made with the same jackknife, and with every sail in working order. Still another time, a homemade bow and arrows, accurate and powerful enough to kill a rabbit or a partridge, although I never used them for that. And there was no new doll, there was a handmade wardrobe for the old one.

But the gifts seem to have been less important than the feasting.

All the great holy days down through history have been feasts. That was true in ancient Greece and Rome. It was true in the Middle Ages, and during the Renaissance. It is true to a certain extent even today. In fact, I suspect that the very conception of the holiday originated in prehistoric times when the hunters came home with meat and the tribe prepared a great feast, a festival.

The adults in that grim place and time must have felt about their chicken and pork much the same way as we children felt about our fruit, nuts, and candy. They were men and women who from childhood had known the sour taste of hunger.

Christmas afternoon, the men drank.

The women, at least in my memory, seem to have spent most of the day looking after babies, of which many of them had several. And they talked, with diaper pins in their mouths, of matters the children weren't supposed to know about. But the men drank. And everything they drank was homemade. Malt beer, molasses beer, spruce beer, hard cider, and the moonshine that tastes like tequila laced with peppermint and nutmeg.

They did their drinking in the barn.

"Come out and take a look at the new cow and tell me what you think of her." That, or something very much like it, meant: "Come and have a drink." Or if there was no barn, and no cow, there was a woodshed. Then it was: "Come and see if you think the bucksaw needs filing." They weren't fooling the women, but then, they weren't really trying to fool them.

Often there was music. Sometimes the only instrument was a fiddle. Sometimes there was an improvised orchestra, whose members, if they chose, came or went in the middle of a tune. There might be a violin, a mandolin, a guitar, a banjo, a mouth organ, an autoharp. Somebody might play the spoons, or the comb and tissue, both of which are precisely what their names suggest. And there would be step-dancing. The first black man I ever knew was a farmhand who vied with my grandmother for the honour of being the best step dancer in the parish. Some of their most spirited competitions took place in our kitchen at Christmas, the two of them facing one another less as dancers than as choreographers—the trick was to improvise new and increasingly complicated movements involving, toward the end, almost every part of the body.

I haven't mentioned the Christmas concerts, at school and Sunday school. The school concerts were opened by the chairman of the board of trustees. Whoever he happened to be, he always looked very uncomfortable and very proud as he flushed, got awkwardly to his feet, muttered something about being unaccustomed to public speaking, and sat down. The teacher, usually a girl hardly out of her teens, although we children thought of her as being as timeless as Megara, bustled about with the preoccupied air of one awaiting the information necessary for a crucial decision. The older boys and girls, scrubbed within an inch of their lives and dressed in their best, looked almost achingly purposeful as they ran about on interminable, unnecessary errands.

At the 1939 concert, I portrayed a soldier doll. Once, at Sunday school, I was St. Joseph. Another time I was Herod.

It was all, when I come to think about it, so very religious. Religious in the subconscious and mystical, rather than in the liturgical and public sense. The Christmas of my childhood belonged to the great tradition, as old as the human race, of holy days and festivals. Everyone sensed that, I think, although hardly anyone ever referred to the formalities of Christianity, its rituals and theologies. Historically, in a sense, it was pre-Christian, the music and the dancing, but in a curious way it was holy. It was the human spirit finding joy in an all but intolerable environment. Even the gods envy man's gift of laughter.

I could have written about other and later Christmases. Like the Christmases when my son was a very small child and I went with him when he looked for a gift for his mother. We went from store to store, and from department to department, him looking for an appropriate gift—except, actually, he wasn't so much searching for a gift as for a sales clerk who could treat him with gentleness and dignity, perhaps even, for the moment, with love. He knew it would be wrong to buy the gift from someone who acted morose or harried or impatient. So we walked from store to store, and from department to department. Until he found a clerk—young or old, male or female, but more often old than young, and more often female than male—a clerk who smiled gently and treated even little boys making one-dollar purchases as though they, too, were members of the human race. Then he bought something, and because gentle, wise sales clerks sometimes sell very odd things, it was often a very curious gift for a mother. But it was purchased in love, as in love it was given.

The Christmas Secret

Gary L. Saunders

In this humorous story from September Christmas, *Gary L. Saunders takes us back to a holiday season when his family celebrated the Christmas spirit by conspiring to hide a warm and fuzzy gift, against all odds.*

Sidney just tumbled into our lives. We had no say in the matter. The week before Christmas, we got this telephone call from a neighbour saying, "Our son has brought home a friend of your son's from Mount Allison University for the holidays—perhaps you could come and pick him up?"

Of course we would. Any friend of our son's was welcome. "But maybe you should wait until the smaller children are in bed," my neighbour added mysteriously. This should have told me something. But as I drove down the road to pick up our guest, I was preoccupied with other things. I remember absent-mindedly wondering where we would sleep this person;

that was all. No doubt, thought I, he would share Second Son's room when he arrived home from university.

As it turned out, this guest would fill the whole house with his presence and make the coming week one of the most suspenseful Christmas countdowns of our lives. For Sidney proved to be youthful, handsome, gregarious, and popular, a Prince Edward Islander by birth, an Allisonian by circumstance, and a prankster by instinct. It was only later we discovered he was addicted to chocolate, fond of booze, loved to chase cats and roosters, and had fleas. For Sidney was a dog.

A Christmas puppy, in fact, with all that this implies. Warm. Fuzzy. Cuddly. Friendly. Stumpy tail wagging while he piddles on your foot with excitement. Big brown eyes and moist black nose. Pink tongue and needle-sharp teeth. Ten weeks old, and chewing on everything and anything to relieve the sting of new molars. And, of course, the inevitable newspaper business—and the business without benefit of newspapers, and sometimes the business without benefit of footwear along the dark hallway in the small hours....

At first we balked, my wife and I, recalling our previous experiences with dogs. We thought of Wrinkles, the boxer-Airedale who disappeared one day; of Max, the mini-Alsatian who got run over and died on our doorstep, and of Tasha, the little Lab who ran afoul of a raccoon trap. "Why a dog now?" our eyes asked helplessly as I returned from my errand and opened my parka to reveal his polar-bear-cub face. I handed him to her, along with his ragged security rabbit. Sidney's tail thumped against her arm. Sidney's face looked up, holding wonder like a cup. "Why not a dog now?" our eyes answered. And that was that.

Except for one thing. How to keep it from the little girls until Christmas morning? "Impossible," I said. "For one thing, where will he sleep? For another, what about his barking?" But Beth had a plan. She had known about him a day sooner than I, and she's smarter anyway. While Sidney drank milk from the cats' dish, she explained. School wouldn't be out for several days, so daytime would be no problem—the pup could have the run of the house. The rest of the time, he would have to stay in somebody's room—with somebody entertaining him when he wasn't asleep. Who would that somebody be?

"Not me," said Eldest Son, home on a visit. "I'm not going to sleep with a dog." Would Youngest Son, sixteen, do it? He would! Eldest Son would have to give up his bedroom, though, for it was the only out-of-the-way space in the house. So it was arranged. As soon as Youngest Son got off the bus each day, he would head for the backroom and puppy-sit until relieved by one of us. To drown out any barking, a radio or stereo was always to be playing, especially in that critical period between when the girls arrived at two-thirty and when he came home an hour later.

I still had my doubts. But somehow—perhaps because everyone loves a secret—it worked. My wife bore the principal burden because she was home most of the time, and besides, it was her idea. Eldest Daughter wasn't too keen on any of it at first. When she first saw Sidney, all she said was: "That ours?" and walked away. Sidney didn't care. He knew he could win us all over, just as he had won over a whole floor of students in Trueman House at Mount Allison, where Second Son had sequestered him for a week in transit from PEI to Nova Scotia.

It was only a matter of time.

Yet how time dragged. Every day was a continuous game of wits.

"Mom, why is everybody going to the backroom so much?" said Joyce one evening. Joyce was seven, and already nobody's fool. "Oh, they're wrapping Christmas presents," said her mother. Which was partly true.

"Mom, I heard a barking noise."

"Oh no, dear. You must be mistaken. Maybe it was the budgie. He sometimes makes odd sounds."

"Yeah, but budgies don't bark."

"Well, maybe someone's been training him to."

One day, unknown to Beth, the clock was a half-hour slow, and the girls walked in before she could hide the pup. Sidney was sleeping under the stove—and they were warming their hands over it. Before he could wake, she whisked them away into the kitchen for milk and cookies, and whisked him in the opposite direction to listen to some loud Chopin until his boy came home.

Christmas drew nearer, as it always does, but slowly, too slowly. Joyce had developed a powerful urge to enter that room. She had to be constantly watched. Why couldn't she wrap presents in there too, she wondered. We put her off with more excuses. And at this point we decided that, since she had been the most curious and was suffering the biggest run-around, Sidney would be officially hers.

One morning near the start of Christmas vacation, in the midst of the daily struggle to catch the bus, Amber, the second youngest, appeared with a look of wonderment on her face. A dreamy nine-year-old, she had run into the room looking for something, and.... "What's the matter?" I said as she drifted by. "There's...a...puppy in the backroom!" she stammered.

"Shhh!" I whispered. "Come here! I've something to tell you." Hugging her close, I whispered the Secret in her ear, and admonished her not to tell her sister. The bus came and off they went, Amber still wide-eyed and Joyce none the wiser.

That day, as it turned out, Amber told her best friend.

The best friend told another friend, and maybe another. But somehow Joyce, three grades below them, never heard—a different grapevine, I suppose.

At last, at long last, it is Christmas Eve.

By now Second Son is home from Mount Allison and is in on the game too. The tension is terrific. On top of all the usual excitement and suspense, there is this time bomb ticking in the backroom, this present which cannot be wrapped in paper but must remain wrapped in mystery for at least a few hours more. The tree is up and decorated, the cakes are baked, the presents are being put under the tree. Now the stockings are hung on the mantel, now the little girls have at last gone to sleep, now everything is ready. The parents drop wearily into bed. The house sits silent in the snowy night.

Soon a light clicks on in the upstairs hall, followed by a patter of feet to our bedroom door. "Can we go downstairs now? To look at our stockings?"

"So soon?" we groan. "Can't be more than three A.M...." Actually it's four-thirty A.M.—not bad, compared to some years we can recall. "Sure, go ahead. We'll be down a little later." And away they go. And we lie in bed and listen for a while and muse on Christmases past, while mentally taping those sweetest of human sounds, the breathless voices of children opening gifts. And gauging the moment for the Secret Gift. The older children are still asleep. We don't want them to miss it. Should we wake them?

There's no need; here come the little girls again, shaking and waking them, eager to open presents, eager to see who got what from whom, anxious to see how we like their own gifts to us. The whole family stumbles downstairs, eight in all, and in the pre-dawn darkness we hunker under the lighted tree and start to open our gifts.

Now is the moment. We bring him out. Sidney licks faces. Wades happily in the sea of noisy paper. Noses the lowest ornaments. Scratches one ear. Plunks himself down to watch.

And we watch Joyce, the object of this week-long conspiracy. Does she squeal with delight? Does she throw her arms around him, cover him with kisses? No such thing. She studiously avoids him. For the rest of us, this is maddening. Perhaps she knew all along? Perhaps she was so sure Santa would bring a puppy that it's no surprise. After all, it was she who, in November, had taped signs all over the house saying, "I WANT A DOG"—signs that we tried to ignore.

We needn't have worried. A few hours later, when the pressure is off, she lavishes on him all the attention a puppy could want.

Since then he has squirmed and wagged his way into all our hearts. He has grown into a handsome golden retriever-cocker spaniel with the gentlest of dispositions and a great sense of humour. Sometimes we wonder how we did without him. Certainly Christmas at our house will need him from now on. Where other Yuletide gifts have worn out or vanished, our Christmas dog is running strong.

Fall and Winter

Evelyn M. Richardson

In this passage from We Keep A Light, *Evelyn M. Richardson looks back fondly on her days spent on remote Bon Portage Island with her young family, as they celebrated a delightful Christmas while maintaining the island lighthouse.*

In any family where there are children, the day about which the whole year revolves is, of course, Christmas, and so it has been with us. We have never possessed nearly as much money as we should wish to spend for gifts, but everything else to make a perfect Christmas we have had.

When I was teaching, always about the first of December I began to develop phases of each subject that stressed the coming holiday season: we read Christmas stories, we made Christmas decorations in drawing periods, and learned Christmas songs in music time. As soon as my own children were old enough for lessons, we followed much the same procedure. As they could see no store windows and took no part in a school or church tree or entertainment, I tried other ways of bringing the Christmas season vividly before them.

I saved all my cards, and so did the children's grandparents; these were passed on to the children the following year, and from them, they cut out lovely designs and made cards to send away, and also little cloth scrapbooks for younger cousins and friends. But most of all, the cards were looked at over and over again and the pictures (some of them really lovely) revealed new beauties and a fresh aspect of Christmas at each inspection. We made transparencies for the windows, and while the children were still too small to do other handwork, we made chains of brightly colored paper links to festoon all our rooms. They were no works of art, perhaps, but the young eyes were not critical, and it was not hard for me to see beauty in them. When the children were big enough to "sew" they did weird and wonderful embroidery on tea towels for Grandma and the numerous aunts—both the real and the "courtesy" ones.

When they reached the age to enjoy "cooking"—and that was still while they needed a chair to reach the tabletop—they cut out cookies in various Christmas designs, baked them, and then frosted them with colored icings. Some of these went to Grandma and Grandpa, who loved the awkward shapes and often slightly bilious effects with the frosting because of the affection and Christmas spirit that went into the making; and a big cookie can of these was part of our own Christmas cheer.

Our stores were the Eaton's and Simpson's mail-order catalogues, and by the time December arrived, the big books were already worn and marked at the pages of cheaper toys and Christmas assortments. The lists that were made and remade! And the multifarious calculations to divide the costs of the larger gifts among the three children in a correct ratio to the weekly allowances (naturally, Betty June, with only four cents a week, say, couldn't be expected to bear the same share of expenses as Lo and Anne with their munificent eight and nine cents) filled reams of paper and hours of Lo's and Anne's time. I was always amazed at how much they were able to purchase with their tiny savings, and how suitably they remembered their little friends and each other—and, with the greatest love and thoughtfulness, Mummy and Daddy. I would make out the order of Christmas supplies (Daddy adding the gift for Mummy), and it went off in the mail early in December. Then came the long wait until a suitable day arrived for Daddy to go off and get the bulging parcel. Unpacking this and distributing the purchase was almost as much fun as unwrapping one's gifts on Christmas Day.

The gifts for folks not on the island must be wrapped and ready for the mail early in the month, and if December seemed to be shaping up as stormy or unsettled, we got our parcels to Shag Harbour before times, often asking the postmistress to hold them until a suitable mailing date. Although I could perhaps have improved on their attempts, I always encouraged the children to do their own wrappings with the festive papers and cords, and certainly the "doing up" of gifts remains one of the greatest pleasures of Christmas. Once the gifts for those outside the family were wrapped and away, we turned our attention to the family preparations.

A week before Christmas Day we put up the chains of colored paper and placed the wreaths and transparencies in the windows, so that the lighthouse began to take on a festive appearance. Most of our friends and relatives, knowing the infrequency of our trips to the mainland and the uncertainty of the weather this time of year, sent their parcels to us early. These soon added another touch foretelling Christmas, and were put in our bedroom for safekeeping. No one would have thought of peeking at a Christmas gift, but it was most interesting to turn a parcel over and about, and to conjecture what lovely joys it might contain! And those that disclosed a rattle or tinkle were the most maddeningly intriguing things! I have said how good our friends and relatives were in remembering us generously at Christmastime, and the contents of the parcels never belied their promising exteriors.

Because our little ones saw no trees in store windows or in the homes of friends, and because we never put our tree up until Christmas Eve and they preferred to take no part in trimming it, we early inaugurated the Dolls' Tree. It was chosen and cut by Anne and Laurie on an afternoon walk, and carried home in triumph; it was always symmetrical, although no taller than would bring the upper branches within easy reach of chubby arms. About the middle of December, it was installed in the same place that the family tree later occupied. Each year, as I put away the Christmas decorations, I placed in a special box any short ends of tinsel, slightly broken ornaments, scraps of gay paper, and cellophane, and these were saved for the doll's tree. All three children spent hours happily making decorations, trimming the tree, and tying up gifts for the dolls and teddy bears. The Dolls' Tree was kept up until we began to clean house preparatory for Christmas Day, when it was dismantled and taken outdoors to make way for the big tree.

Getting the Christmas tree was the occasion for a family outing. We all bundled up in warm clothing and went along the path and through the woods, stopping at every likely copse of spruce and fir, and passing judgment on the individual trees. At last we would all agree on a likely conifer and Morrill would begin to chop it down, while we stood breathless until he had taken that first decisive cut, and then watched every step of the felling with mounting excitement. Our trees are large, from six to eight feet tall, and with amply spreading branches. While Laurie was too small and no hired man was with us to take one end, Morrill pulled the tree, still vibrant and resilient, on Laurie's sled, over snow or bare ground as conditions dictated, along the path, over the hill, and home to the shed. While he prepared the base, we hastened to move things in the kitchen and living room so as to clear a place before the western window.

Then came the bustling and squeezing and pushing to get the tree through the doors and upended, while the crisp cold perfume of its branches filled the room with awakened memories of all the Christmas Eves we ever knew, all the tremulous thrill of being about to touch briefly something too lovely, too sweet, too good and heavenly to bear touching; of becoming, for a few hours, part of the miracle, and sensing in our own hearts, tight with joy and love, the birth of a new world of peace and goodwill to all men. Once the tree was in its place, we all fell quieter momentarily, as if it brought the calmer joys of Christmas with it, and its submissive branches spoke to us for a few fleeting seconds of the sacrifices that buy us happiness. After the tree had been decked with its ornaments, we forgot the hush that had fallen upon us when we first beheld it upright and beautiful in its appointed place.

I always tried to keep Christmas Eve as quiet as was possible with three little ones almost bursting with joy and excitement. After the supper dishes were put away and everyone was scrubbed and shining, came story time, and the stories that had come to be regarded as the special ones for Christmas were rather an odd collection and are now gradually being outgrown. First the Christmas story of the Bible, so full of beauty and wonder; then *The Night Before Christmas*, jolly and rollicking; and next a rhymed tale of three orphans who lived on an island off the coast of Maine, and whose Christmas dinner was lost when their boat capsized but who made out marvelously with a baked cod. (It is not hard to understand why this jingle appealed to our three little islanders.)

Another favorite was a *Family Herald* story about a poor little girl whose Christmas had to be postponed till New Year's, and then was of the scantiest. I don't know why this became a favorite, except that it aroused their pity, and Christmas should be, as Dickens says, a charitable time when we remember those less fortunate than ourselves. Finally, I finished by telling a story I remembered from my teaching days, a tale of how Santa sprained his ankle and Mrs. Claus substituted for him. This was greatly beloved, and when it was done, three sleepy youngsters hung up their stockings, previously selected and marked with vari-colored strings for quick identification, and were ready to go to bed. Though many years have passed since the first Christmas on Bon Portage, we keep the Christmas preparations as little changed as we can with the growth and development that the years bring to the three youngest members of the family.

Every parent who has filled a stocking or trimmed a tree knows how we spend the remainder of the evening; the happiness with which we place each gift upon the tree, seeing, in imagination, the light across the beloved little faces as the Christmas joys shall unfold for them in the morning. If we have a hired man with us, he takes part with us in trimming the tree and placing the gifts, and shares, as much as lies in our powers and his, the family spirit of Christmas; and it is part of the fun to keep the children's awkwardly tied gifts to him out of sight as he works about the tree.

Often we are able to get lovely Christmas music over the radio, and its poignant beauty fills the cozy, lamplit room where the tree sparkles in its tinsel and flashing balls. Like all the world, of late years our hearts have been saddened particularly at the Christmas season for the plight of unhappy millions, but we feel we can do no good by curtailing the happiness of our children; although we pare to a minimum the money we spend, so much of our Christmas cheer costs nothing but time and love. The uncertainty of the winter weather makes it impossible for us to share our Christmas with young servicemen away from home, as we have so often wished we might.

No modern silver and blue or other chastely restrained color schemes are found on the Bon Portage trees. Like the ones I remember from my childhood, our trees are as gaudily and glitteringly bedight as we can manage, and I even have some of the crimson balls that enthralled me as a child, passed on to me when the family tree at Bedford graduated to electric lights. We often use candles, because we feel the fire hazard is small when we remember the green, wet tree so recently cut.

At last, when the final ornament and gaily wrapped gift is placed, and the stockings bulging, Morrill and I pause for a moment to enjoy the scintillating sight before our weary but happy eyes. We never tarry long, for we know the hours are few before the fun begins.

Long before the lazy winter sun is up, we hear voices, tense with excitement and happiness, in the rooms above us, and the steep stairway creaking under eager feet. Then whispers and happy squeals and indrawn breaths of pure delight come from between our open bedroom door and where we know the tree stands, half-revealing, half-concealing its treasures in the gleam of Laurie's flashlight. But the gifts on the tree are for later, so a dash is made for the stockings behind the stove. We call out, "Merry Christmas, kids!" to let them know we are ready to join in the mirth. Then comes a mad rush for our bed, and three pairs of icy feet are thrust into the erstwhile warmth between our blankets as three bathrobed youngsters range themselves against the footboards and pull the lower ends of the bedclothes over them. They suffer the illusion that we are all covered and warm under this arrangement, and we listen to the happy chatter as they unpack their stockings and strew our covers with the contents.

The year that Betty June was three, the other two tried in vain to arouse her to the same pitch of excitement they were experiencing. Betty June just couldn't remember anything about Christmas, and wasn't greatly interested; even hanging the stockings seemed not to impress her, and Anne and Laurie were in a terrible state of impatience and frustration, and tried to arouse her interest with detailed accounts of all Christmas held. She remained maddeningly imperturbable. But on Christmas morning, it was quite a different story—she arrived in our room, blue eyes aglow and tousled curls perky with excitement. She took her place at the foot of the bed and proceeded to unpack her stocking. Viewing each item with surprised glee and mounting ecstasy, she placed it near her as she enumerated:

"I told you Santa would bring me a dolly."

"I told you Santa would bring me candy."

"I told you Santa would bring me grapes,"

And so on through the dates, nuts, figs, and raisins, to the orange in the toe. Then, in one long-drawn sigh of satisfaction, she looked around at the circle of our amused faces and announced in triumphant conclusion, "I told you!" And such is the power of the Christmas spirit that even Laurie forbore to say, "You never said a word," though I saw him stop it on the tip of his tongue.

We never dare to leave a fire overnight, because the flues are none too safe and because of the tremendous drafts when the wind breezes up, so on Christmas, as on all other winter mornings, the rooms are chill, and Morrill gets up first to make the fires. Soon the living room is cozy, and the little ones depart for its warmth with their treasures to reexamine them between attempts at getting dressed.

The rule is nothing from the stockings, except grapes or an orange, is to be eaten before breakfast, so they all eat a fairly hearty meal, and this is a great help in preventing upsets later.

After the necessary morning chores are done, we spin out the opening of the gifts as long as possible. Morrill takes the presents from the tree and Betty June, as youngest, distributes them. Then each of us takes a turn at opening a gift while the others watch and admire. This system possessed great advantages when the children were too small to remember which kind friend or relative had sent which of the many gifts unwrapped, for it enabled me to keep a list for future acknowledgments.

Unwrapping the gifts takes most of the morning, and then I must hasten to the kitchen to prepare dinner. We have never had turkey, nor do we miss it. Goose, both wild and domestic, ducks, also of both kinds, and chicken have all at various times provided us with our Christmas dinner. For dessert we have a steamed carrot pudding (the recipe for which has been in our family for generations) served with whipped cream, and, of course, the usual extras that go with Christmas.

Seldom do we have a white Christmas, but always, if the weather does not absolutely forbid (and I remember only one such Christmas Day), we go for a skate or a long walk after dinner. This makes a welcome break in the surfeit of goodies and excitement, and we arrived home hungry enough to do justice to a supper of cold meat and a bottle of extra-special preserves, as well as the time-honored fruitcake.

After supper we light the candles on the tree, then play some of the new games or read one of the books invariably found among our gifts. We all go early to bed, perfectly happy from a day that has brought us many welcome gifts and assurances of love and care from friends and dear ones, a knowledge that though we are apart from them and cannot join in their Christmas cheer, we hold a place in their minds and hearts, and this is the best part of Christmas. It was at Christmastime during our first years here that I missed most keenly the fun and companionship of a large, boisterous family and the friendships and social gatherings of pre-marriage days.

We keep the tree up till New Year's, and then we reluctantly dismantle it. The children were allowed, when very small, to take a part in this; they prefer not to share in decorating the tree, but to see it first in all its glory in the early hours of Christmas morning, but they admire each ornament as it is taken from the tree, gently wrapped, and tucked away for another year. We are by no means weary of the happy glitter and spicy perfume of our tree, but school lessons must be resumed immediately after New Year's Day, and the tree and greenery must be put away to welcome a clean and busy New Year.

When I started to write, I thought I would like to pass on to the many young couples who will, I hope, be building their lives along the northern frontiers and other isolated spots, much good advice on how to be happy and to find compensations for the isolation, the lack of companions and of many amenities that have made life easy and interesting. That must have been the schoolteacher in me cropping up again. After all, only the same main ingredients go to making a happy marriage and a full and contented life wherever circumstances place a young couple. Everything is included in these two—hard work and love.

A Coal Miner's Family Christmas

Andy MacDonald

These three hilarious passages from Bread & Molasses *explore the intricacies of growing up poor at Christmastime in Cape Breton.*

1 Duck—2 lbs.

11 children—1500 lbs.

Ma and Pa—300 lbs.

Total Ma and Pa and kids—1800 lbs.

Amount of duck each consumed—1/555 lbs., and still hungry.

OK, MY POOR DUCK

That feeling of Christmas for a child is one he'll never have again. Just to hear the word "Christmas" spoken was a thrill, even in July. A week before Christmas we were at our best, willing to do anything for any member of the family without argument. A few days before Christmas, Pa would give each of us a dollar bill to buy something for ourselves. How we appreciated that! What great affection we had for Pa, who had been so rough on us throughout the year.

Billy was the slickest of us all. He would always buy Pa a good, substantial present, not with thoughts of love, but speculating on a gift from Pa that would cost much more than his. With the Christmas spirit spreading over us, we'd go to town next day to look over the toys.

Our scheme was to buy as many gifts as a dollar could buy, without taking too much of the dollar. I bought a metal duck with a winder on it. When wound, the duck would flap and quack. It cost sixty-nine cents, but for the first few days, it was priceless. As soon as I'd open my eyes in the morning, the duck would be on my mind. I guess I thought too much of it. The greatness of it couldn't go on forever. One morning, Teddy walked on it with a pair of heavy shoes and cut off all circulation to the quack and the flap. We tried everything to repair it.

I can still see the look on the duck's face, as though it were suffering pains and aches in its crushed tin body. But Teddy had a frog that croaked and jumped when you wound it. Nowadays, in retaliation, a brother might jump on the frog and behead it, but that never crossed my mind. I just wanted half-interest in the frog in return for the damage inflicted on my duck. Since the duck was ground-born for good, all my attentions went to the frog. It was constantly on my mind. Teddy then issued a bulletin that he would wind him twice to my once. I accepted this, and things were going wonderfully for a few days. Then one mild day in January, when Teddy was nowhere in sight and snow was scarce, I figured the frog would do better outside in the wide open spaces. So I took Mr. Frog outside for his first outdoor show. I'd wind him up and watch him croak and leap. I was so interested in this marvellous frog, I forgot about eating. I devoured all his actions instead. I was thinking about my good fortune in having this frog all to my-self outdoors when I saw the coal man coming with his horse and cart. I had to open the gate for him and his horse.

Seeing a horse was a real novelty; I forgot all about the frog and concentrated on the live horse, watching the way he knew where to go and what to do automatically. The coal was dumped, and the horse took his roundabout course to turn. I watched, spellbound by the sight of his muscular rump, while those big cart wheels, spoke by spoke, went over Teddy's frog. In seconds, that shapely frog was completely round. The shock was tremendous. It was so severe that I forgot to shut the gate. I kept wondering, "What can I do to make it look like a frog?" But nothing I could do would help its condition. Soon Teddy arrived on the scene, and when I presented him with the round frog, he went into a state of shock, not realizing I was just coming out of one. He cried and cried, while I frantically tried to form a frog or anything out of the shambles I had adopted half of.

Eventually our sorrow spent itself, and we pooled the remainder of our dollars. We had eighty-two cents between us to shop with. That was big money in those days. Then we got a terrific idea. We decided to buy a live rabbit; in fact, the man who sold them gave us two for our money, and said to take good care of them like he did. He couldn't have given them to better owners. We would have breathed for them if that were possible. Home we came with the rabbits, anxious to make them a perfect home. The white one was to be Teddy's, and the brown and white one mine. Sleep meant nothing to us.

We had live creatures to take care of. They ate much better than us for a while. Not having much time to make them a home before dark, we took them to an old henhouse and fixed up a temporary place for them. Teddy's white rabbit was a lovely sight to see. Even to me it was the head of the party, and so we gave it the best place in the hen barn. I arranged a place for mine up over a few boards, which would do until the morning when we could make a better place.

Early next morning Teddy and I went out to see our love-ables. I found my brown rabbit stretched out full length. A board had fallen during the night and struck him squarely on the head. This was a rabbit punch that would have been fatal to any rabbit. Teddy's rabbit was in paradise, while a calamity had fallen upon mine. We gave him a burial Pope Paul would have received. We prayed at his funeral, placed him in a box, and marched him to a special place in the garden. Ashes to ashes and dust to dust were sprinkled, and the lid softly closed over him.

We didn't mourn the rabbit's death for as long as we normally would have, because we had Christmas to look forward to.

I'm Jack Spratt, But She's Too Fat

In school, the Christmas tree concert was a great event. A tree was mounted and colourfully decorated. At school we appeared happy and joyous, but at home calm and collected, owing to the fact that Pa was never affected by this good cheer until a couple of days before Christmas.

I was unfortunate enough to have Mrs. Brindel for three different grades, and while the teachers with love for the Yuletide were lining things up for their party with recitations and transferring pretty pictures of reindeer onto the blackboard two weeks before Christmas, Mrs. Brindel was telling us to take out our geography books. This, to us, was like smoking around a gasoline pump.

When the door was open and the room drowned with Christmas songs from the other classrooms, she'd slam the door hard as if to say, "Humbug! Let's get on with our work." She would have been the ideal teacher for grades one and two, to explain to the five- and six-year-olds why there was no Santa Claus. She might even have gotten out a chuckle.

A few days before Christmas, she'd let her hair down and start rushing out a few plays here and there, but even this never made us like her any better. She'd never want any of us to laugh or to catch her laughing.

I was never the type to be picked for a play—only playing behind the scenes, like thumbing my nose at her when her back was turned. But somehow, this one year I ended up with a recitation from the old goat a few days before Christmas—not knowing who my partner was until the last minute. Hardly having time to memorize my loving part, I was fortunate enough to have heard it about a thousand times from nursery rhymes out of the only book of rhymes we had, passed down from four generations. It was the old story of "I'm Jack Spratt, I can eat no fat, my wife can eat no lean, but between us both, on Christmas Eve, we lick the platter clean."

There I was the day of the play, sitting with my empty platter, all aired up to shout my piece, when I turned to see this large creature coming from behind me, floor creaking. I held off my recitation, waiting for this ungodly heavy person to be seated or continue out the door. Instead, she threw her large parts up next to me and gave me a sort of "Hi!" look. Here I was with an empty platter, sitting across from the fattest, homeliest girl in the school, with me doing all the talking, as she had no part to say—just sit there with her fat body and a stupid look on her face. I even kind of edged away as if she didn't belong there.

Why hadn't the teacher told me I was to have her as my wife? Surely, seeing the same kids every day for a full term, the teacher must have had some knowledge of who liked me insofar as flirting was concerned. Why, then, did she match me up with a character three times my size, knowing full well she'd be the last person I'd have an interest in? Nervously, loudly, and swiftly, I recited my part, then flew to my seat amid thunderous applause, which must have been for her, as she was still sitting there.

At those concerts, parents would circle the desks in chairs to hear what their sweet little girls and boys were saying as each recited a small verse. Some kid tensely waiting to perform would walk urgently to the centre of the floor, only to find out he had suffered brain damage on the way and had forgotten every line of his verse—all eyes focused on him. With head dropping just a little towards the floor and a quick sixty-degree sway, a tremendous cry would fill the room, ending in dry sobs. Sometimes these sobs stuck around as long as two hours after you had had a healthy cry. Clapping never helped the situation, as the kid would think, "Hell, I never said anything yet and I don't want pity." Had I not gone through this, I wouldn't know how to explain it. Why, I was raving and raging for a week or so, showing how I was to come out in front of those spectators. But when the crucial moment arrived, all motors stopped; my sobs appeared and stayed around even a week after the outburst.

At those Christmas parties, some big shot's daughter would say her piece so low in volume that even if you'd had your ear clamped to her mouth, you wouldn't have known what she had said, but the applause she'd get would almost blow her off the stage. Up I'd go, knocking pencils and papers off the desks I passed, with my large jacket open and swinging, heading for that certain spot on the floor where the first thing to be noticed by the multitude was my attire. Not caring for the eyes analyzing me, I'd say my piece at the top of my lungs, sometimes roping it out so fast and loud there would be spit accompanying it landing on my chin.

Steering clear of those Christmas plays became my objective. "Mary or Jan can play that part better than me." Besides, what if Pa came to see it; why, I'd frizzle up like a lizard when you put salt on him, if I were to say my part and look up to see Pa smiling. Either he or the crowd would get an object thrown at them.

Bobskates Aren't For Swimming

Weeks before the time for the stockings to be hung, when Ma and Pa were visiting neighbours, we could read each others' minds. With Ma and Pa only a few feet out the door, Bill would take us to the hiding place under an unused, darkened cupboard. We didn't go there too often, as we were told it was a rat hideout and we could get a nasty bite in the dark. As we got older, Bill got the nerve to check.

This one Christmas Eve, four pairs of bobskates were found. There was a large pond a hundred feet from the house, an ideal place to try them. We forgot that it had been unseasonably mild for the last few days; before us lay four pairs of skates. At two A.M., with the house in silence, we slithered out of bed like baby snakes. Almost walking on air, so as not to make too much noise when our weight hit the twelfth step and it creaked, downstairs we crept. We spied our skates again, which were now sitting under our stockings, which hung on three-inch nails so that Santa could leave each of us one hundred pounds of his loot. (A claw hammer was placed nearby to pull out the nails as soon as the stockings were taken down, in case Pa might brush up against them, tear off half his shirt, and ruin our Christmas.)

The skates were put on in silence. Led by Bill, we raced to the pond. Though the morning was dark, we found one small path, and with a formidable thrust, we all followed Bill out onto the darkened pond. The ice, about one thousandth of an inch thick, wouldn't have held a beam of light—yet here we were, following Bill at breakneck speed until we reached the other side, a distance of two hundred feet. Taking the skates off, we tried to dry them with our shirttails. Then, skates over our shoulders and sock-footed, we took the land way home. There, more drying was administered in silence. The skates were placed back under our socks and off we slunk to bed.

Feeling too damp to sleep, we whispered until eight A.M. Then we heard heavy footsteps, and we knew Pa was in motion. Like sweetly behaved kids, we followed him downstairs, trying to make a scene of gleeful surprise as in the old English plays. Luckily, Pa fell for our act and advised us how we were to take care of our skates by drying them off thoroughly after use, not knowing we had baptized them six hours before on the pond.

From Causeway, A Passage From Innocence

Linden MacIntyre

Award-winning author Linden MacIntyre recalls
his early boyhood memories of the holiday season
in rural Cape Breton.

Christmas is the one time of the year when money doesn't seem to matter. Gifts and food appear as if by magic. Worries disappear.

I ran for home with news of the COD from Simpsons, the dog ahead at first, but then doubling back to urge me to go faster, swinging behind me and passing me repeatedly, whirling in excitement because he knew as well as I do what Christmas means.

The COD is the conclusive sign, but the weather is always the first indicator. After Halloween the trees are bare, leaves that were red and gold and orange all through October are now congealed in soggy, rotting piles that are, on chilly mornings, covered with a furry-looking frost. Cold rains flatten the dead brown grass in ditches and in the fields. The chilly air is heavy with the smell of fermenting apples.

The week before Christmas, the dog and I will go to the woods with an axe, the way we always do. Over the hill and past Jack Reynolds's, where there used to be a stagecoach depot. Past Alex MacKinnon's, where the railwaymen sit in their undershirts on the doorstep on the warm summer evenings. Past Mrs. Eva Forbes's, the widow who has plum trees in her yard, and a big piano that she sometimes lets my sister Danita and her friend Annie MacKinnon play on. All the way out through Big Ian MacKinnon's back field.

We follow a track that probably was once a road, around the edge of the field, past a clearance that used to be a farm they still call LaFave's, until we are now behind the cove where they used to quarry gypsum. I pretend that the axe is a rifle and that we are Indian scouts, defending our village from all the white explorers. I would like to get a real rifle for Christmas, but I'm probably too young. The house could use a rifle, I believe, for when he isn't here.

There is a high waterfall that crashes over ice-encrusted rocks at the bottom. I go carefully around that obstacle, and then back on the path that leads to Happy Jack's Lake. Red squirrels chatter and rabbits dive for cover in bushes, with the dog darting after them.

The lake is frozen. The older boys believe it was formed by a meteor from outer space and that it has no bottom. They skate there when the ice gets thick enough. I have skates, but they don't fit me yet. They belonged to a miner who was killed in Newfoundland. My father told me I can use them just as soon as my feet are big enough to fill them. I asked him what happened to the man who owned the skates, and he says he'll tell me someday when I'm older.

Near Happy Jack's Lake, as usual, I'll find the perfect tree. The dog will bark in approval as I chop it down, feeling the glow of knowing I have done the man's work and that my mother and Grandma Donohue will rave about it.

Then we'll open the door of the dining room to let the heat in.

And one evening, when the room is warm enough, we'll stand the tree in a corner and decorate it. On Christmas morning, I will join my sisters in their bedroom, which is just above the dining room, and we'll look down through the hole in the floor of their room to see what's there, underneath the tree. It will still be dark, but we have a secret way for turning on the light that hangs on a wire in the middle of the ceiling. It was my invention, the first Christmas after we got electricity in the house: I tie a string to the chain that turns the light on, run the string down and through the rung of a chair, then back up through the hole. Early Christmas morning, we gather round the hole. I pull the string. The room is suddenly illuminated. We take turns peering down, figuring out who got what. Then I pull the string again. The room, with all its Christmas riches, is lost again in darkness. We return to our beds and begin the long wait for daylight.

Once my father showed me a large photograph of a group of men in rubber working clothes and with lamps attached to the fronts of their hard hats. That was in Newfoundland, he said, where I was born. The miners were standing in front of the headframe, everybody smiling and looking full of mischief. "This," he said, pointing to one of the men, "is the one whose skates you inherited."

The dead man was standing beside my father with a big grin on his face and not a clue that he would soon be gone.

And now it is Christmas, and this year he won't be coming home because he's already here. He is our father again, no longer just a visitor from somewhere else.

It Had to Be a Fir Just the Right Size

Trudy Duivenvoorden Mitic

In a series of interviews, three Nova Scotian senior citizens lovingly recall their real-life memories of Christmastimes in the first half of the twentieth century.

Memories are made of people, places, and occasions. Perhaps the Christmas season, more than any other time of year, affords the opportunity to collect precious memories and harbour them zealously to savour at some future time.

Perhaps also, it is the serenity and joy of Christmas that gives rise to the ready recollection and outpouring of poignant memories of seasons and celebrations long since past.

Annie DeWolf Trites, a 101-year-old resident of Saint Vincent's Guest House in Halifax, delights in recalling Christmases spent as a youngster in the 1890s.

For young Annie, who lived with her widowed mother and three siblings in Liverpool, one of the first signs that

Christmas was in the air was the making of corned beef and mincemeat in late fall.

As the festive season approached, her mother, a resourceful woman on a very limited income, would become more and more secretive, busying herself with mysterious tasks. Finally, to the delight of her children, she would announce in mid-December that the time had come to set out in search of a tree.

Although there were trees available for sale in town, Mrs. Trites recalls that, "Mother was very fussy, and so cut her own. It had to be a fir, just the right size and shape. It was exciting for us to go with her."

Accordingly, the young family hired a horse and driver from the local livery stable, and made its annual merry pilgrimage to the outskirts of town in search of the elusive perfect tree.

Mrs. Trites hastens to explain that in those days, if you saw a tree you liked by the side of the road, you could simply chop it down and take it home. Such action was common, and never thought of as vandalism or stealing.

Once the selected tree was brought home, it disappeared into the parlour, not to be seen again by the children until Christmas morning.

When the great day finally arrived, breakfast was downed in a hurry and the eager children were led to the parlour doors. Then they were flung open to reveal a splendid tree, which stood from floor to ceiling, meticulously trimmed with a variety of homemade and store-bought decorations.

Always, a fire glowed warmly in the parlour fireplace. To the unrestrained joy of the children, a new homemade toy for each could be found under the majestic tree.

As well, for the girls there was always a new hair ribbon, and a dress made by their mother from material provided by a thoughtful relative.

There was also certain to be a box of Christmas treats from a kind friend or cousin. Lastly, each child looked forward to receiving a small cake, carefully decorated with his or her own name.

Mrs. Trites recalls that Christmas in those days was a family time, spent quietly and intimately at home. Dinner was always a delicious affair, complete with roast chicken and plum pudding.

Later in the day, as she did on many a Sunday afternoon, Mrs. Trites's mother would gather her excited children around her and read to them, perhaps from the Bible or perhaps an excerpt from a novel that she herself was currently reading.

To the children, the choice of material wasn't nearly as important as the opportunity to enjoy their mother's kind and soothing voice.

Mrs. Trites remembers those days with affection in her heart. It was a time when the importance of family reigned supreme, and emphasis on material goods and money was minimized.

She does, however, recall the one small extravagance that the family joyously indulged in every Christmas until all of the children were grown; each year, a very special ornament was lovingly selected and purchased to add to the family's cherished collection of tree decorations.

Alex Penny, a 94-year-old Haligonian, vividly remembers Christmas as celebrated by his family in the 1920s.

He and his late wife, Winifred, and their only child, Pauline, relished in the holiday preparations as well as in the actual festivity of Christmas.

While Pauline impatiently awaited the arrival of Santa, the Penny home was decorated with holly and mistletoe. At least a half-dozen plum puddings were made, to be served later to family and friends.

The tree, fruit of an annual family expedition to the then -wooded Rockingham area, was trimmed with ornaments and numerous little candles. (Although the city homes of that era had electricity, a string of Christmas tree lights was then still a thing unknown.)

The tiny candles added a special sparkle to the season, but Mr. Penny now confesses that he was "always afraid" of the fire hazard that they represented. Hence, the candles were eventually abandoned in favour of the safer, more modern electric tree lights.

On Christmas Eve, after their daughter had reluctantly retired to bed, the Pennys arranged gifts beneath the tree and filled a stocking with treats and tiny toys. This, they slipped onto Pauline's bedpost after she had fallen asleep.

Did Mr. Penny ever play Santa Claus?

"More than once!" he chuckled, adding that he had his daughter soundly fooled for a number of years. As Santa, and in an improvised costume, he would make a quick and sudden burst into the child's room as she was preparing for bed. Seconds later, he would disappear, leaving the youngster wide-eyed with wonder and excitement.

Early on Christmas morning, the delighted Pauline would pounce upon the contents of her stocking, her peals of excited laughter bringing contented smiles to the faces of her parents.

After a quick breakfast, the Penny family would attend a worship service at their church, an important part of their Christmas tradition.

The turkey dinner would be enjoyed at midday, and afterwards the gifts would be brought forth from under the tree and opened. For Pauline there was always a special gift from Santa; perhaps a shiny new sled, a bicycle, or a pair of ice skates.

Mr. Penny remembers Christmas Day as being a family celebration. During the holiday season, however, numerous friends visited and enjoyed games of bridge and impromptu dances on the hardwood living room floor while feasting on holiday treats.

In those days, Mr. Penny maintains, Christmas was not nearly as elaborate and as commercial as it is today. In those days, rather than relying on restaurants and nightspots for their holiday entertainment, families did their own feasting and celebrating.

Ask Sylvia Doyle of Halifax about Christmas during the war years, and her eyes grow large and misty with recollection. The widow of Patrick John (Jack) Doyle, Sylvia poignantly remembers Christmas in the years between 1939 and 1943. Those were the years when Jack, who had enlisted with the Royal Canadian Air Force, was unavoidably away from home at Christmastime.

In her husband's absence, young Sylvia strove doubly hard to make Christmas a joyous occasion for her four small children: Peggy, Jean, John, and baby Christine.

Sylvia was adamant that the family traditions that had been developed in previous years would nevertheless be continued during this trying period.

On Christmas Eve, the children gleefully sifted through their bureaus in search of the longest, most stretchy cashmere stockings they could find to hang from the mantle. They then prepared a glass of milk and a plate of homemade cookies for Santa to enjoy, a task in which they took pure delight.

After the youngsters were finally and reluctantly settled into their beds, the Christmas preparations began in earnest. With the help of a houseful of relatives and friends, the tree was put up in the living room and trimmed with homemade ornaments and strings of popcorn and dried cranberries.

Amidst the hushed chatter and laughter, Sylvia and her guests decorated the house, assembled toys, and nibbled on treats.

Occasionally, when the volume of the merrymaking grew loud enough to drift upstairs, someone would playfully admonish the group not to "awaken the kiddies."

Sylvia does not remember the children ever waking up during those nighttime festivities.

Before retiring to bed at four o'clock in the morning, Sylvia's last task was to fill the stockings and place them at the foot of the children's beds.

The stockings were always religiously filled in the same order: first a big, juicy orange was stuffed into the toe. This was followed with an apple, a handful of nuts, some deliciously sticky candy wrapped in wax paper, and a clear toy. Finally, a special item was placed into the top of the stocking—a tiny doll or teddy bear, or perhaps a miniature jack-in-the-box.

Sylvia tenderly recalls that, "the screams of excitement between six and seven o'clock, when the stockings were found on the foot of each bed, were worth being up until dawn."

Although the young father's absence was felt poignantly on Christmas morning, the undaunted Sylvia was determined that laughter and good cheer would nevertheless reign throughout the house on that day.

After church and a hurried breakfast, the excited brood, led by the eldest child, was ceremoniously assembled in front of the closed living room doors. Finally, after what seemed like an endless wait to the little ones, the doors were thrown open to reveal a wonderful tree set amidst a magnificent array of colourful packages and shiny new toys.

In late afternoon, Sylvia and her children, along with her brothers and an assortment of other relatives, assembled at her parents' home for the Christmas dinner. The crowd delighted in the turkey, the plum pudding with lemon or hard sauce, and the variety of homemade pies all generously topped with whipped cream. A highlight of the Christmas table was the fruit bowl, filled with a variety of fresh fruit scarcely available during the rest of the year.

As the end of the day neared, a very special and long-awaited telephone call finally came from the beloved Jack. Cries of "Merry Christmas!" and "We miss you!" rang throughout the house as Sylvia and the children crowded around the telephone receiver.

Christmas Day ended with a hope and a fervent prayer that Daddy would soon be coming home.

Were those years a time of financial hardship for the Doyle family? Sylvia does allow that money was scarce and had to be prudently spent. As well, staples such as butter were still being rationed, and thus the Christmas baking had to be carefully planned well in advance. Items such as fresh fruit were a rarity to be savoured only at Christmastime.

Sylvia has generous praise for her family and friends who provided her young family with a marvellous support system during the years that Jack was away. A steady stream of visitors, especially during the Christmas season, ensured that loneliness and despair would not be allowed to envelope the Doyle household.

In the years that followed, five more sons were born to Jack and Sylvia Doyle. Today, Sylvia is the energetic head of a family that includes seventeen grandchildren and six great-grandchildren. It is a family that zestfully continues to enjoy the holiday traditions that were begun so long ago.

As yet another Christmas season draws to an end, this one also filled with highlights, tender moments, and special occasions, new and equally precious memories are committed to the wondrous storehouse of the mind. On some distant future day, they too will be fondly recalled and lovingly retold to help fuel the fire of the perpetual wonder that is Christmas.

Recollections of Christmas Past— The Gaspereau Valley

Norman Creighton

During the 1960s and 1970s, Norman Creighton was a celebrated CBC radio broadcaster. In this passage from Talk About the Maritimes, *he recounts the special pleasures of celebrating Christmas in a Maritime village.*

Imagine Christmas—without any money! We are back in the year 1900. The place is the Gaspereau Valley in Nova Scotia. You are ten years old, growing up on a farm. You have been in to Wolfville once, in the cutaway sleigh, and gaped at the Christmas finery along Main Street, glistening in the store windows. There were toy drums in red and yellow, china-headed dolls, a railway steam engine with a cow-catcher in front, a fire engine drawn by two white horses, a jack-in-the-box, a rocking horse.

Probably, none of these will be for you. Perhaps the jack-in-the-box, possibly the toy drum; but the rocking horse or the railway locomotive, no. Your parents have not encouraged you to write a letter to Santa Claus, confiding that one of these might perhaps interest you. Yet you have a feeling, a restless, breathless intimation, that something spectacular will be there waiting for you on Christmas morning. Else, why did your parents not allow you to accompany them into the general store? They have no money to buy things, of course. You know that. But they do have credit, built up over the months with baskets of eggs, prints of butter, and bags of turnips and potatoes.

The door opens and your father beckons you to come in. You throw back the robe, bound out of the cutter, and next moment you are inside the store, standing beside a hissing beehive stove, surrounded by barrels of fancy biscuits and caddies of tea. The shelves are piled with crockery and yard-goods, and on the counter is a rounded glass case filled with candy.

Your mother hands you an egg. You, in turn, pass this egg on to the merchant, who now indicates that you may pick out any candy in the case. What a choice! There are saw logs, six inches long, in solid peppermint, chocolate tents with cream centres, and conversational lozenges: "You are my sweetheart"; "Can I see you home tonight?" in the most poisonous shades of pink, yellow, and purple.

During the long drive home, you lie curled up on the floor of the cutter under the buffalo robe, chewing on your peppermint saw log, listening to the chiming of the horse bells, dreaming of all the wonders you have seen, and speculating if Santa Claus might bring you a pair of larrigans, as he did last year to the two boys who live on the farm halfway up the mountain. They each received a pair of larrigans and a poleaxe! They could hardly wait for Christmas dinner to be over before they were out tramping back to the woodlot to try out their new axes.

Then you begin thinking of Christmas dinner. There will be mince pies. The very choicest of mince pies, made with rabbit meat from rabbits you caught yourself back on the mountain, because everyone knows that rabbits make the best mincemeat.

Your mind is irresistibly drawn back to those strange-shaped parcels your father has stowed away in the back of the cutter. What will they contain? You are on the verge of reaching back to see if you can touch them, when the cutter suddenly stops. You look out from under the robe, and here you are on the river road, almost back home, alongside the neighbour's mailbox. Your mother hands you a cup and gives you careful instructions. There is baking to be done today, and she will have to borrow a cupful of seed yeast from her neighbour's supply, to start off a fresh batch. This will be poured into the big stone two-gallon yeast jug, and placed beside the kitchen stove to ferment. Of course, she will return the cupful later on, when her neighbour's yeast jug begins to run out. By the time you get home with the yeast, the mysterious parcels have been whisked off into the house and are nowhere to be seen.

Already your mother is at work seeding raisins, for she now has some kidney suet she got at the store. Only beef kidney suet, the very best, will do for a plum pudding. Everyone gathers about to take a hand. Each member of the family gives the pudding a stir, for good luck. But first, Grandpa must recite the riddle, the traditional jingle which he teases us with every year.

Flour of England, fruit of Spain,
Met together in a shower of rain.
Put in a bag, tied around with a string,
If you tell me this riddle I'll give you a ring.

The answer, of course, is a plum pudding. When the pudding is cooked, your mother takes the pudding bag, washes it out, dries it carefully, and stores it away in the pantry for next year.

Is there to be a Christmas tree? Perhaps, but not likely. The Christmas tree was brought to Canada not too many years before, in 1846, by a German woman who married Mr. William Pryor of Halifax. This was the first Canadian Christmas tree, and though the custom spread rapidly, in 1900 there are still many homes where it is frowned upon, particularly in communities with a Puritan background—and the people of Gaspereau Valley originally came from New England.

But there are decorations! You and your brothers and sisters have been busy for days making tissue paper chains, and wreaths of ground juniper for the window, decked out with wild holly berries and crowned with a homemade tallow candle. You have been doing immense things with pine cones. These were painted with ordinary house paint, red, green, and white, and frosted with sugar and salt before the paint hardened. Grandpa watched benignly over all this activity from his rocker beside the wood-burning kitchen stove. Every so often he lighted his pipe and, as this was Christmastime, Mother offered him a match from the book of wooden matches she had purchased at the store, matches tipped with sulphur. But he shook his head. Grandpa prefers his own self-made spills. He keeps a supply of these on the mantel, and after he has lighted his pipe with one, he leans over, snuffs it out among the ashes, and returns it to the mantel for future use. He sits there with his jackknife, fretting pieces of wood into the most curious shapes. Whatever is he making?

At last it is Christmas morning. Now you know that Grandpa has been busy making a dancing man—a little wooden man with jointed limbs, hanging from a cord strung between two poles, who will dance for you when you give a rhythmic touch to the cord.

There are other presents too, most of them homemade: hand sleds, a little wheelbarrow, a tiny dump car, a pair of spring skates. Then, for the girls, there are pinafores, stocking caps and mittens, and a yellow hair-ribbon for one, blue for the other.

On Christmas Eve you hung up your stocking, not forgetting to set out a plate with an apple on it for Santa to give to his reindeer, because nothing sustains reindeer like an apple grown in the Gaspereau Valley.

In that stocking, this morning, you found an orange, an openwork bag of gumdrops, a tiger or an elephant made of clear candy in yellow or red, and a toy: for the boys, a tin whistle, for the girls, a rag doll.

Your presents occupy you completely all morning until you hear the oven door being opened...and there sits the goose, the hot fat sizzling in the pan, the smell of sage dressing perfuming the air. Not only is there a goose, but the roast of pork as well, with applesauce to go with it—all grown on the home farm.

As your father carves the goose, everyone watches to see the state of the keel bone—a most important and urgent matter, this business of the keel bone. For if the keel bone is white it means a heavy winter lies ahead, with much snow. But if the keel bone is partly white and partly dark, you can look forward to an open winter and an early spring.

Whichever colour it is, you know there are plenty of supplies stored away in the cellar, and a long winter ahead to play with all those toys. You will learn to skate on your new spring skates—and who needs any money?

Father Christmas Unmasked

Nellie P. Strowbridge

This wonderful story from The Gift of Christmas
*tells of the first coming of Father Christmas to a
small Newfoundland outport on Christmas Eve.*

Gertie grew up in the 1920s in Island Cove, a small
outport with a beach lapped by the sea. On a high-rise
strip of land was a spread of saltbox houses flanked by
woods holding thick fir trees. No one thought to bring
the trees indoors and decorate them. There were no coloured
lights. Only the soft glow of lamplight filled windows in cozy
homes, their fires fuelled by firewood. The cove people had
seen a sketch of Father Christmas only on Christmas cards,
and not often.

The small, isolated community, reached only by boat or
horse and sleigh, had no Christmas catalogues. But word had
gotten out that there was a Father Christmas,2 and that he
brought gifts to children on Christmas Day.

"Twasn't like it is now," says Gertie, "with Santa Claus in every mall. The only *maul* we knowed anything about was the kind used to drive a stake in the ground.

"Sure, there's no Christmas like an old Christmas. We had fun down in Island Cove. We had Christmas for twelve days. Now kids got it from September to January, but it's all harassment, everyone wondering what to buy everyone else, and how to better the other person with the best present. When I was a girl, a schooner showed up in the spring of the year to take Father and the rest of the men in the cove to Labrador. They went by sail, with the wind taking them where it wanted to, with only glasses to go by. They were gone from June to September, and when they finished fishing in the fall of the year, they came home with the fish salted down. They spent all fall washing and drying the fish on flakes. Besides that, we had a horse, a cow, sheep, and pigs, and we grew our living on the point. When the fish was cured, the men packed it back in the schooner and took it to St. John's. The skipper took half of the voyage, and the merchant took half of what was left for the fishermen.

"The men sailed back home, then they and their women left for Northern Bight Station (Goobies) to catch the train to St. John's for winter supplies. They brought back ever so many pounds of rolled oats for three cents a pound. They unloaded wooden boxes of tea, and butter, barrels of flour, kegs of molasses. We'd have raisins, and sweets in wrappers to be kept for Christmas. The men brought back four- and five-gallon kegs, with molasses sugar on the bottom, as cheap as dirt. They used the molasses sugar and yeast to run off moonshine for the Twelve Days of Christmas. The moonshine was made after midnight when no unwanted visitor was likely to show. We had a back door that led to the woods, should the moonshiner need to make a quick run.

"Preparations were made around the house inside and out. Cakes were baked, heavy and succulent with raisins, spices, mixed fruit, rum, and molasses. The scent of Christmas baking went all through the house, rising up the stairs to bedrooms where the children lay dreaming of getting something in their stocking."

By Christmas Eve, Gertie and her brothers and sisters were all excited about Christmas Day. The Christmas dinner: a male goat or a pig was slaughtered. Sometimes a goose or a turkey was killed and plucked. Kindling was stowed in porch lockers, the hunting guns were placed in their racks, and the homemade wine, birch beer, and moonshine were ready. Hooked and braided mats were washed and dried, and floors were scrubbed. Then, after the family had finished a scoff of molasses bread and boiled salted salmon, their mother cleaned the stove and iron kettle with black polish. She stirred her kettle of berry hocky and strained it into cups, sweetening it for a delicious drink. Vamps were hung on the bedposts for the children. What was in each vamp sometimes served as the only Christmas gifts.

Christmas Eve was only the beginning of a twelve-day season to look forward to. With the wood laid in and the moonshine out, the men went on the idle, while the women still served and mopped pools of water and mud behind company who spent the night in booted dances, cracking jokes and telling ghost stories and riddles while helping themselves to a taste of the missus's hospitality and the mister's grog. Children watched adults become children again, and dressed up for the best bit of fun they had all year, laced with a bit of Christmas cheer.

One Christmas Eve, Gertie and her siblings got a big surprise when a knock came on the door. No one in the cove ever knocked on anyone else's door before walking in. The only knocks anyone had ever noted were a succession of three raps. Such an event foretold the death of a person in the community. This time there was only one knock, and then the children all looked up as a strange figure filled the porch. In the soft lamp-light that shadowed the porch, a figure standing in front of the children was an imposing sight. The creature was dressed in a red robe, and wore a white cloth over his face and a black cap.

Gertie wasn't old enough to know that the real Father Christmas always showed his face. This figure came like the first Christmas mummer of the Twelve Days of Christmas, but he didn't speak like one.

"Ho ho ho!" he called. The children looked shocked at the sight of Old St. Nick so close. Except for Gertie, who was sit-ting on the inside of the table with Uncle Ike (who lived with the family), all the children scampered upstairs to get away from the masked man, whose *Ho ho ho!* followed them. Gertie squinched when Father Christmas came into the kitchen, close enough to hold out a handful of candy. She was scared, think-ing that maybe it was one of her neighbours dressed up. He had killed a pig, and when she saw him scraping it, he threatened to take out the pork chops and sew her up inside the pigskin.

She cautiously reached out her hand; then she pulled it back.

"Go ahead," Uncle Ike urged her. Then he looked at the man and said, "Knock off your foolishness with that child," as if he was acquainted with the stranger. Gertie thought him bra-zen to speak in this manner to Old St. Nick. For sure he would never darken their door again after such an unwelcome! Father Christmas ignored Uncle Ike and held out his hand again. This time, Gertie cautiously lifted a candy from his hand. Then he thumped his way upstairs. Gertie grinned, imagining the children leaping on their feather beds and moving against the wall, afraid of him.

Father Christmas coming as the first Christmas mummer on Christmas Eve became a tradition. If the children were upstairs when his black-mittened fist hit the door, they would all come running back down for candy. From under his red outfit, the old fellow pulled candy from a bag and filled each little hand. Norman, Gertie's younger brother, wanted more. He held out both hands. Father Christmas filled only one. Then he left.

Cyril, Gertie's older brother, was bolder than the other children. He scoffed at the idea of Santa coming in a sleigh hauled through the skies by reindeer. He wasn't sure he believed in reindeer either. He had never seen one. One Christmas, he decided that it was about time Old St. Nick showed his face. He was sure Santa was nothing more than a common mummer from the cove. He hit upon a bold plan. That Christmas, the children sat on the bed waiting for the old gent's step on the stairs. When he came into the bedroom, the girls squealed.

Old St. Nick reached out his hand with candy, and when the candy was safely in Cyril's hand, Cyril reached out his other hand to grab the false face. From Father Christmas's gait and the look of his boots, Cyril had gotten suspicious. He had unmasked Arthur Will, the children's father.

"I knowed 'twas he," Cyril called in triumph.

"Could be his twin," Beatrice, his youngest sister, said, not willing to give up Old St. Nick. Father Christmas beat a hasty retreat down the stairs. "Now we've lost our treats," Annie wailed. "We'll find them in our stockings," Cyril promised. The next morning, there were sweets in each stocking.

Gertie remembers a red ribbon in hers, used to tie a red bow in her hair.

Father Christmas didn't show his face, masked or otherwise, in the cove ever again, but the mummers did. They came knocking loudly and screeching, "Any mummers allowed in?" When they got in, they ordered a tip of moonshine, which was given only after they threw up their false faces.

Gertie, now eighty-eight, is well and spry. Just as night is scattering on Christmas Eve morning, she is in her kitchen cutting up salmon and codfish, and peeling potatoes for the thirteen family members coming for supper. When she finishes her work, she sits for a spell. She leans back in her chair, folds her arms and says, "I always said that Cyril took Santa Claus. We missed him, we did. But we still got the candy. The only thing that changed was that Father stayed in the house all Christmas Eve.

"Now Father is gone. Annie, Cyril, and Norm are all gone. Santa Claus—he's around yet. Still, there's no Christmas like an old Christmas."

A Woodstock Christmas Eve Long Ago

Alistair Cameron

Alistair Cameron immigrated from Scotland with his parents to the Upper St. John River Valley in 1929. His first years in the village of Debec, Woodstock, and along the river are portrayed in this passage from Aberdeen It Was Not.

The main street of Woodstock is crowded. It is the evening before Christmas, and people with glad faces, eager shoppers every one, stop and turn to gaze upon the miracle of crimson, green, and blue lights hanging on the Christmas tree in the town square. Breezes sway the branches that have bowed low under the snow, and children with sweet and wistful faces peek underneath to see if Santa is there. They do not find him, and yet in their eyes shines the hope that generations of men have stumbled through to find the dream that is Christmas.

In the old days, to go to town on the day before Christmas was a sheer necessity, or so we thought. All afternoon, horses hauling pungs with jingling bells, loaded with cheerful and excited families, came to town, to become caught up in the festivity of the season. Wives carrying baskets of butter, freshly churned, and covered neatly with snowwhite tea towels, made a beeline for George True's grocery store, or to Yerxa's, or Hall's, or wherever loyal customers were in the habit of trading. Husbands followed close behind, with dozens of eggs carefully packed in oats and placed in half-bushel measures. Plucked geese had been brought to town earlier in the week. The butter and eggs were a sort of afterthought, a little bit extra, for this was the time to forget about pinching pennies. This was the day and the place to meet old friends; so we gathered, young and old, to walk up one side of the street and down the other seeking out treasures, often with very little money to spend. But there was always a smile and a hand clasped tight, raising Christmas above a surface experience as the goodwill in our hearts gave us deeper faith and stronger hopes.

In Jones's Music Store, just across the Meduxnekeag Bridge, a record player with a loudspeaker attached played carols, lending an air of happiness to the shoppers crowded around the door to listen to the sweet strains of a long ago shepherd's serenade. In other shop windows, and in houses close by, lights glimmer, and garlands gleam in gold and silver. We drink in the beauty of it all while thinking of our own humble, candle-lit tree and the dim glow of the kerosene lamps at home.

In Jacob Brody's store, always a favorite meeting place, we greet each other. Old men with their pipes firmly grasped between teeth that have seen better days, talk and puff, sitting on chairs thoughtfully provided by Mr. Brody. Overhead, rows of fleece-lined bloomers and ribbed woolen stockings, hung by ropes from the ceiling, flutter and wave from the heat of the old wood stoves. Men who will never be too old to feel the glow of Christmas look over the gum rubbers and felt slippers, silently counting the cost, and concluding that Christmas is worth it.

Around on King Street, the Farmer's Store is bursting at the seams with people from all over. The store has a "shut up" smell about it, but it is a good smell. The aroma of well-cured cheeses, apples, oranges, ointments, and disinfectants mingle with the smell of perfume and powder that lingers over the group of women who, standing by the candy showcase, laughingly exchange recipes and talk about mince pies. On the counter hereby, boxes of dry codfish, one box of which is open, are given the "go by." The smell of salt and sea just can't compete with the exotic fare of Yuletide, which is tastefully arranged on shelves and tables throughout the store. The phone on the wall rings. Everyone for miles around knows the number 6-6. Someone wants to speak with Mrs. Cunningham, who is brought to the phone with much bantering and laughter. Silence descends as she talks, and everybody soon knows that a neighbor wants her to bring home a bottle of cascara and three whole nutmegs. A weariness is on the clerks as they cheerfully dash to and fro. They know that the peace of Christmas morn is not far off, and they will be glad when this day is over and the night has quietly slipped off to its bed.

Back on Main Street, the trek begins all over again. Young men in groups pretend to ignore the girls who pass by, and yet, in their hearts, they long for that one word that will break the ice. Instead, girlish giggles fill the air, and, for once, that glorious spirit of Christmas seems to have escaped; but only for a short while, for one of the girls finds a way and, directed by her heart and guided by much goodwill, graciously wishes the bashful young men a "Merry Christmas." Then, with happy and faster beating hearts, they all wend their way to Newnham and Slipp's Drug Store for cups of hot chocolate.

The Salvation Army band, gathered in front of the Carlisle Hotel, draws people around it. Common folk have turned from shoppers to worshippers as they listen to the stern old melodies and happy Christmas hymns woven together in memories of other seasons such as this. It has been a long time since the first Christmas lullaby was heard by the baby, pillowed deep in a manger on a stable floor. When the plate is passed around, hard-earned nickels, dimes, quarters, and dollars are gladly given. Men, women, and children are conscious of where the true spirit of Christmas really dwells.

Children gaze in awe upon a manger scene in the Manzer's Store window. High in a corner, a tinsel star glows as a silver beam sheds light upon it. The straw on the stable floor looks just like the straw in the barn at home, but here, somehow, it looks different. It has a sacred look about it. As the children stare with wistful eyes, mothers and dads in the background remember their own childhoods and wisely shake their heads, knowing that their own faith and hope will live again in their children, to be passed on to future generations; for only a child can truly feel, see, and hear the real meaning of Christmas. The street is beginning to empty now. The day is fast drawing to a close. The songs of Christmas can still be heard from the loudspeaker over the door of Jones's Music. The listeners gradually turn away, eager to start for home and the warmth of the old kitchen stove, where dying embers are soon coaxed into flame. In Patten's Drug Store, there is a last minute rush for boxes of chocolates. The box tops with their rustic scenes are a present in themselves, and will make a nice picture for some lucky girl's bedroom wall.

In Daye's Barber Shop, Jack Daye brushes the hair from the shoulders of his last customers. The till gives a "ping" as the quarter fee is deposited. The patron, sheared for the holy day, departs amid a chorus of jolly greetings. On the sidewalk, he pauses to pull up the collar of his jacket and then, taking a whiff of the frosty air, he smells the bay rum hair lotion and does not regret the extravagance of having this finishing touch added. After all, this is the season of frankincense and myrrh, so surely his wife will overlook this indulgence.

On the corner of Main and Connel streets, lads scarcely in their teens shiver as they peer into the window of Aliotis Bros. Store, wondering what they can buy for a quarter. They decide on a tin of tobacco for dad, and a comb and bobby pins for mom. They enter the shop to spend their meagre mite, happy in the thought that it is better to give than to receive.

The lights in Selrite's Five and Ten are turned off, and the clerks come out, bundled up against the cold night air. They turn weary steps towards the cheerfulness of home.

A tired little fellow, wearing pants that are too long for him, comes trudging along. A big smile lights up his face as we pass. He is proud of his purchase, and he clutches the scented cake of soap in a mittened hand. Some kindly soul in Sib Balmains has carefully wrapped it up for him in multicolored paper. The gold cord tied around it reflects the light of the street lamp as he places the bow to his lips and smiles again.

At Lutze's Hotel, the stable caretaker has had a busy day. Customers are straggling in, and soon the stable will be empty. Men, more subdued now than they were an hour ago, hitch horses to pungs, and then wait patiently while wives and children make themselves comfortable with soapstones and buffalo robes. In the warm stable, an old radio crackles and wheezes before a voice, deep and clear, fills the gloom:

"Let us accept the gift sent to us so long ago so, that our hearts on Christmas Day may echo the song that a heavenly chorus sang, 'Peace on Earth, Good Will to Men'."

A shower of blinding snow comes tumbling down and just as quickly as it comes, it stops. Once again the radio snaps and crackles, and then the voice of Lily Pons rings out in a tune as old as the hills:

"And blessed be His glorious name to all eternity, the whole earth let His glory fill, Amen, so let it be." After that, there is silence. Silence above, and silence below, on a Christmas Eve in Woodstock a long time ago.

Christmas At Sea

Stanley T. Spicer

In this passage, revered nautical writer Stanley T. Spicer explains the unique marine traditions that were developed and practiced by sailors who spent their time at sea during the holiday season.

In this December of 1961, the signs of Christmas are all around us. In towns and hamlets along the St. John River, among the highlands of Cape Breton, and beside the tides of Fundy, stores are crowded and homes are readied for the festive season. In King's County and Queen's County, Saint John, St. John's, and Charlottetown, mail sacks are heavy with parcels and cards, and the wreaths and lights cast their glow from a thousand windows. But these are only the man-made symbols. The real celebration of Christmas is in the music of the carols, the anticipation in the face of a child, the story of the birth of Christ. For many of us, Christmas is a time for family and friends. But in the unfolding pages of time, man, in his endless search for utopia, has found many ways and many places to spend this season of the year.

Much of the history of these Maritime provinces is related to the men and women whose destiny lay upon the sea. These were the people who built and manned the windships, and forged a new era of economic prosperity for the young country of Canada. It was an era complete with full measures of success and failure, triumph and tragedy; and as we turn back the pages of time, we can find revealed some of the experiences of these seafarers during their Christmases of long ago. These were not the good times ashore, but the days and months at sea that illuminate the never-ending struggle against the elements.

The annals of the sea record many stories of incredible hardship, bravery, and loneliness. To the men, and their wives followed, the sea Christmas was often a wintry period on the stormy North Atlantic, or a sweltering day in the South Pacific. Sometimes there was tragedy. It is not difficult to picture the scene aboard the barque *Happy Home* as it neared the Nova Scotia coast in late December 1880. Captain Hiram Coalfleet, master of the Hantsport-built vessel, had with him his wife and daughter, and Christmas had been a happy family event. Then a few days later, in a January gale, the *Happy Home* struck the dreaded Trinity Ledges off Yarmouth. Mrs. Coalfleet and her daughter were lashed to the rigging as the barque pounded herself to pieces. When assistance arrived, the captain and surviving members of the crew were removed to safety. But for Mrs. Coalfleet and her daughter, Mary, it was too late. They had frozen to death.

Then there was the new full-rigged ship *Welsford*, of 1,292 tons. In December 1856, on her first voyage sailing from Saint John to Liverpool with a cargo of deals, she ran ashore at Cape Race, Newfoundland. The captain and twenty-three members of the crew lost their lives on Christmas Day.

Sometimes Christmas meant a day of incredible hardship. On December 11, 1868, the little schooner *Industry* left the LaHave River for Halifax, only fifty-four miles away. On board were the captain, Lewis Sponagle, the vessel's owner, Ronald Currie, three seamen and two passengers, one a pretty young girl, Angeline Publicover, who was going to Halifax to buy her wedding dress.

All day, in a light breeze, the schooner sailed toward her destination, and shortly after midnight Sambro Light, guardian of Halifax Harbour, was sighted. Then, without warning, a storm beat down upon them. Entrance into Halifax was impossible and the *Industry* turned to run back to LaHave. In the process, the foresail split and the kerosene can upset. There was no more light for crew or passengers. As the schooner neared LaHave, the gale shifted again and drove the vessel out into the Atlantic. For three days and nights, they ran under bare poles. The deck load of cordwood on the wildly pitching schooner was somehow tossed overboard, but a water cask was struck and smashed. Soon only two gallons of water remained. Salt water seeped into the food supply, and for two weeks those on board sustained life on ten hard-tack biscuits. The pounding of the seas started the seams, and the vessel began to leak. Constant pumping was necessary to stay afloat.

Christmas dinner was celebrated with one soggy, raw potato cut into seven pieces. Finally, the exhausted crew could no longer man the pumps. On December 29, when hope was gone, they were sighted by the barque *Providence*. The *Providence*, under Captain Hiram Coalfleet, the same mentioned earlier as master of the *Happy Home*, effected a daring rescue, and less than an hour later the *Industry* sank beneath the waves. The rescued were taken to London and then returned to Nova Scotia, arriving on February 12, sixty-three days after leaving

LaHave for the short sail to Halifax. Thus, a small group of Nova Scotians escaped Atlantic storms with memories of a Christmas they would never forget.

Another Christmas of hardship is recorded in the story of the full-rigged ship *Milton* of Maitland, Nova Scotia, and her courageous master, Captain Henry MacArthur. December 1881 found the ship sailing across the Pacific towards San Francisco. Captain MacArthur had with him his wife, Kate, two young sons aged four and two, and a total crew of nineteen. On December 22, fire was discovered in the cargo of coal and a desperate fight to save the vessel began. On the morning of December 23, they were forced to abandon the ship. Three small boats were provisioned and a course was shaped for the coast of California, some twelve hundred miles distant. When Christmas morning dawned, it was discovered that one of the boats had disappeared during the night. Its occupants were never seen again. A Christmas meal was fashioned from the limited provisions aboard the two remaining boats for survivors, wet most of the time from seas shipped aboard, and constantly under the hot equatorial sun.

Early in January, the mate's boat also disappeared and now the captain's boat sailed on alone. On their twenty-seventh day, the water supply was exhausted, but the ingenious MacArthur rigged a condenser from old cans, which provided slightly over a pint per day. For eight adults and two children it was just enough to stave off madness, but death soon appeared. Frankie, the youngest child, died on his mother's lap crying for water. On February 5, one of the crew died. The next day, land was sighted, and a small schooner came along and picked up the survivors. Thus ended an ordeal of Christmas and forty-four other days for the captain, his family and the crew of the ill-fated *Milton*.

Occasionally, Christmas witnessed triumph on the seas. On July 4, 1852, the famed Saint John–built vessel *Marco Polo*, under command of Captain James "Bully" Forbes, left Liverpool for Melbourne, Australia, with nearly one thousand emigrants. Before sailing, Forbes boasted he would have his ship back within six months, considered impossible at that time. Forbes knew his ship, and he knew the south latitudes, and he drove the vessel, making the passage in sixty-eight days. Leaving Melbourne on October 11, the *Marco Polo* arrived in the Mersey River after a record round voyage of five months and twenty-one days. Christmas of that year saw the *Marco Polo* flying a huge banner, upon which was painted "THE FASTEST SHIP IN THE WORLD."

Then there were the mysteries of the sea. Early in November 1872, the little brigantine *Mary Celeste* sailed from New York for Genoa. On board the Spencer's Island–built vessel were Captain Benjamin Briggs, his wife and child, two mates, and a crew of five. On December 4, less than a month later, the *Mary Celeste* was sighted several hundred miles off the Azores by a passing vessel. Because she was sailing oddly, the *Celeste* was boarded, and there was not a living soul to be found. Although the weather had been bad in the area, it was not sufficiently so as to cause undue concern. Clothing, food, and personal effects were all there. The log was complete to November 25. How did the captain, his family, and the crew of the *Mary Celeste* spend Christmas in that year of 1872? Were they alive? No one knows to this day.

To those who followed the sea, the ports of the world were familiar points of call. Captain Joshua Slocum, the Nova Scotian who became the first man to sail alone around the world, knew well these ports. During his three-year voyage in his thirty-six-footer, he knew storms and danger—yet he too could celebrate Christmas. In 1895, on Christmas Day, he was comfortably berthed in Montevideo. The next Christmas found him in Australia, after a dangerous voyage through the Straits of Magellan and across the broad wastes of the Pacific. In 1897, he spent Christmas Day in a roaring gale off the Cape of Good Hope.

Two men on the ship *County of Pictou* never forgot Christmas Eve in the year 1879. On a passage from England to Philadelphia, the vessel was running before an easterly gale. Late in the afternoon of December 24, the captain was forced to heave to. Murdock Morrison of Dalhousie, New Brunswick, was at the wheel, and Peter Carroll of Pictou was on his way aft to assist. Just then, a huge sea broke over the stern, smashing everything in its path. Both men were washed overboard, finding themselves some twenty-five yards away from the ship. Then they were caught in another sea, lifted up, and washed back to the vessel, where they were able to grasp the rigging. Morrison suffered a broken leg and the ship was so badly damaged that on the following day, Christmas Day, the crew were taken off by a passing steamer, and the *County of Pictou* was set afire and abandoned.

Thus it was, time and time again. Today we prepare for another Christmas, and the brightly decorated trees, the lights, and the tinsel are making their annual appearance. Those who will be spending this Christmas with families and friends listening to the carols and to the laughter of children can be thankful. It was, and is, not always so.

Early Christmas Customs in Nova Scotia

Phyllis R. Blakeley

One of Atlantic Canada's most noted historians recalls the unique Christmas traditions that were developed and maintained by many of the early settlers who first came to the shores of Nova Scotia in the eighteenth and nineteenth centuries.

Over the years, many races have settled in Nova Scotia, bringing different Christmas customs with them. For the French, Christmas is a sacred day, with its impressive midnight Mass at the parish church, and its *réveillon*, a special repast served on their return from church in the early morning hours. At Chezzetcook, the Acadians ate a Christmas dish called *garteau*, consisting of birds, rabbits, and pork with a pastry top, which was made in a long pan. Then they sang, danced lancers, polkas, and waltzes to the tune of a fiddle, and played the card game so popular in Nova Scotia called "forty-fives." All slept late on Christmas morning, and spent a restful day visiting the neighbours, singing old French carols, and telling stories. The day for exchanging good cheer and gifts was New Year's.

The English people brought their customs of merry-making with them from the old country. It was the custom in English farmhouses to have mince pies and plum puddings, and a large cake called the yule cake; to light an immense candle on Christmas Eve; and to put on the fire a huge block of wood called the yule log.

The light was said to represent the glory that illuminated the field and shone about the shepherds in their night watch. Many Yorkshire people settled in Cumberland County, and there the table is spread on Christmas Eve with pork pies, bread and cheese, elder wine, and ale. This was much enjoyed for only a pudding called *furmity,* made of new wheat boiled in milk, had been served for breakfast and supper. About midnight, the village singers burst forth beneath the windows, and the master of the house let them in. It was considered unlucky for anyone but a black-haired person to enter the house first. In one village, an old man, who had headed the musicians for thirty years, always took the lead, although his black hair had become as white as winter snow; but no one dared mention this to him!

In Essex, on Christmas Eve, groups of dames in red cloaks and lace-trimmed black bonnets wandered over snowy fields to different farms asking for gifts. This custom was retained in many parts of Nova Scotia, where the young people dressed in costumes like we do now at Hallowe'en, and went from door to door begging for the poor, and singing carols. They were called "maskers," or "mummers," or "waits."

In Halifax in the 1820s, lads in weird costumes visited from house to house. The children stood fascinated while the "maskers" acted a short play, which ended with a duel fought with much clashing of staves until "Jack" fell dead. Then the doctor felt the pulse of the victim, and poked him smartly in the ribs while reciting a mysterious invocation. Up sprang Jack! Then the "maskers," or "Christmas boys," were regaled with Christmas dainties and rewarded by a few pennies. The newsboys on Joseph Howe's *Nova Scotian* newspaper wrote a poem, and distributed this broadside with the holiday edition of their paper, as their Merry Christmas to Halifax.

To Lunenburg County, the German settlers brought the custom of *Belsnickling* (a corruption of *peltznickel*), and dressed in disguise, they went looking for treats, recalling the European feasts of Saturnalia and the later mummers' plays. In the old days, the men wore ox hides with horns and tied bells round their necks. Naughty children were supposed to be whipped with the ox tails, while good children were rewarded by gifts of cakes, fruit, sticks of candy, apples, doughnuts, and other presents. No work was done between new and old Christmas, except for preparing meals and the necessary chores around the farm. Dr. Helen Creighton has described in her *Folklore of Lunenburg County* how some groups carried ox bells or other instruments to make a noise, and that at Mahone Bay, a group played a tambourine, violin, autoharp, triangle, and mouth organ. Their music was so highly regarded that later, the party telephone lines were kept open so that people in other villages could hear them!

"Coburg Cottage" in Halifax is supposed to be the scene of the first decorated Christmas tree in Canada, then the home of Mr. and Mrs. William Pryor. Mrs. Pryor had been a German lady named Miss Barbara Fosse, and introduced the custom from her native land in 1846. However, Prince Albert had recently introduced the decorated Christmas tree into the English court, and this may have inspired Mrs. Pryor to adopt the same custom from her native land. Decorating the tree meant making chains of coloured paper, and stringing rose hips, cranberries, and popcorn balls. There were tiny coloured candles fitted into metal holders and clipped to the tree, throwing their soft light over the room. Glass ornaments imported from Germany could be purchased at a few Halifax shops.

A feature of the festival for the Sunday School of St. John's Anglican Church at Lunenburg on December 26, 1866, was that a large tree stood in the centre of the schoolroom, lit up with wax candles, and decorated with confectionery and other Christmas gifts. On both sides of the room were long tables "groaning under the weight of tea, coffee, plain and iced cake, and a large variety of other articles," and this tea was followed by hymn singing and speeches. Other Sunday schools had Christmas concerts.

Not everyone celebrated Christmas. The Puritans, descendants of the Puritans of Cromwell's England and of New England, brought with them their belief that it was a crime to celebrate Christmas. Of course, the Puritans had lost control of England long before Halifax was founded by Governor Edward Cornwallis and 2,400 settlers from England in 1749, but several thousand transplanted Puritans from New England came to the capital of Nova Scotia. These people believed that the celebration of the nativity of Christ was attended with much more evil than good.

Simeon Perkins, the Connecticut merchant who had settled at Liverpool and who kept a diary for over forty years, reflects the Puritan attitude. For the Perkins family, Christmas was a day to attend church, and to return to a large family dinner—to which a few friends might be invited. There was no mention of gifts being exchanged. By 1804, the Puritan spirit had mellowed sufficiently for Colonel Perkins to allow his daughters to decorate the chapel with evergreen. It was an ancient tradition that Christmas greens had magical powers to keep evil spirits out of the house. But Christmas Day was still occupied by church services and a family dinner.

In the early days of the history of Halifax, those who wished to went to church on Christmas Day; but the unpleasant truth is that the majority stayed at home and got drunk. There is a story that at one Christmas dinner, thirty kinds of wine were served, and one old dame tasted them all and walked from the table as gracefully and erectly as she had approached it! The entire day was spent in feasting, merrymaking, and house-to-house visiting, with coasting and sleighing and skating in the afternoon for the younger ones. Tobogganing on Citadel Hill became popular.

The main course of the Christmas dinner consisted of goose roasted with pork and applesauce, or good old-fashioned beef floating in its own juices, with poultry as a side dish. This was topped off with grapes, nuts, sugar barley candy, fruitcake, and wine, and a plum pudding wafted to the table on lighted brandy. It was an old English custom to put a ring, a thimble, and a piece of money in the pudding while it was being stirred. The one who found the ring in his portion was the first to be married, the one with the thimble was to be a bachelor or a spinster—at least for another year—and the one who received the money was to expect more.

One of the most brilliant entertainments ever held in Nova Scotia was the Christmas ball and supper given by Governor and Lady Wentworth on December 20, 1792. The whole house was open, and every room illuminated. The company was assembled in Government House at eight o'clock, and a large and excellent band played "God Save the King" three times over, after which the country dances commenced, two sets dancing at the same time. There was a room set apart above stairs for cotillions, with a special band for those who liked this kind of music. During the dance, special refreshments called *orgeat* and *capillaire* were served. (*Orgeat* was a syrup of barley water with orange flower water, and *capillaire* was a syrup of maidenhair fern, flavoured with orange flower water.)

At midnight, the ladies sat down at the table in the supper room and were waited upon by the gentlemen, who tripped around in their buckled slippers and long, curled wigs. Among the decorations on the table were models of Hartshorne and Tremaine's new flour mill at Dartmouth, of the windmill on the Common, of the new lighthouse at Shelburne, and of "the tract of the new road from Pictou." When the ladies left the supper room, the gentlemen sat down to drink loyal toasts with the governor, while a tune was played after each bumper. At two o'clock, the dancing recommenced, and the company did not begin to return home until four A.M.

Most of us think that all the talk about how a belief in Santa Claus is harmful for children is the product of modern psychology, but articles similar to those of today appeared in the nineteenth century. In the *Nova Scotian* of 1844, the editor, Richard Nugent, was reminiscing about his boyhood Christmases, and how he and his brothers and sisters had played "hunt the slipper" and "blind man's buff" on Christmas Eve, and the joy of reading "Jack the Giant-Killer," for Charles Dickens had not yet written *A Christmas Carol*. Their stockings were filled with gingerbread, nuts, fruit, and candy. Now, his children came running into the bedroom at dawn shouting: "Papa, a Merry Christmas" with their hands filled with the fairy-tale gifts of the kindhearted Santa Claus, who was so benevolent to little boys and girls at Christmastime.

The green market was an important part of Christmas in Halifax in the nineteenth century, for Haligonians visited the market square near the ferry wharf when the air was spicy with evergreens, and there selected a Christmas tree from the hundreds of graceful firs covered with powdery snowflakes. The city market was so small that the country people sold their goods on the streets surrounding the post office, and the mayor worried about women and children being exposed to storms. Country women sold eggs, butter, cream, poultry, vegetables, knitted mitts, and socks, and did their Christmas shopping in town with the money. It was usually the menfolk in Halifax who came to the market to select the turkey, goose, pair of plump chickens, or rabbits for the family Christmas dinner.

In 1858, it was already an established custom for families to make a tour of the "downtown" streets in Halifax to admire the windows in jewellery stores, dry goods shops, and even the hardware establishments. This custom continued till after World War I. The confectionery store windows were heaped with fruit and nuts, and with candy clear-toys—in the shapes of pigs, horses, cows, rabbits, and firemen—and with striped candy canes five feet long! "Pa" scarcely had a moment's peace till "Mamma" and the fair ones, with him for a chaperone, "explored Granville, Pleasant [now Barrington], George, Hollis, and other streets on which the sights are to be seen," wrote the editor of the *British Colonist* in 1858.

In the newspapers of a century ago, there were no Christmas advertisements such as those that besiege us today. The same ads ran for a month without a letter changed! There were no advertisements of credit, or to hold any purchase until Christmas Eve, and no offer to buy in 1865 and pay in 1866.

In 1865 the American Civil War had ended, but there was fighting in New Zealand, and Fenian raids in Canada. Lincoln, Palmerston, and Cobden had died, and the Atlantic cable had failed. Queen Victoria, still grieving over Prince Albert's death, left Windsor Castle with the youngest members of her family for Christmas at Osborne on the Isle of Wight. The Prince of Wales (later King Edward VII) returned from the funeral of his great-uncle King Leopold of the Belgians, to spend the holiday with his wife and two sons at Sandringham. Prince George had been born that year, and he was destined to spend many Christmas seasons at Sandringham as King George V, and to broadcast his Christmas radio messages from there.

Christmas a Stone's Throw From the Sea

Lesley Choyce

In this passage from Driving Minnie's Piano, *celebrated writer Lesley Choyce recalls a Christmas full of thoughtful contemplation on Nova Scotia's Eastern Shore.*

Jody barks at everything, anything—an exercise of opinion and sound, a soundtrack for the snow with the wind collaborating. The sky, a scud of grey-white clouds, and the wind from the north, of course. A touch of east maybe, taking the dryness from the snow and giving it a subtle touch of weight and character. The uninvited snow is cold against my bare ankles; then back inside to plug in a kettle, and wait for the kids to find daylight and slip groggy-eyed into the kitchen. In front of the house, on the long, frozen slab of lake, the snow does not settle, but finds the slick, flat pane of surface and races off south to clutch at the bushes in the marsh, to fashion white dunes that mimic the ones on the nearby beach.

The day will go slate grey, dark like a bruise, or settle into something vivid if the blue behind the shroud above has the courage to save us. I pour the tea and settle into a near-silent meal as I long for something from the past, some nameless thing that probably never was; but it is there nonetheless. It mostly concerns time. The passage of time; the infinite loss of things slipping through my fingers this morning over a bowl of cornflakes, a mug of dark tea. Nothing—not a thing wrong here, just the fact that I can't hold onto any of it. Each day is flying away as this one will. I want to say this out loud, but I remain silent, sipping at the steam above the cup like it is a vapour of hope.

And so the day begins. Winter in Nova Scotia. Two days before Christmas and I, for one, am glad this is not the holiday, for I do not trust holidays. I trust the average day, the everyday. The day like this, with the dog barking now to come in and be fed. I test the cold again as I open the door, sense it is not as hostile as it first seemed. More snow pours in, the dog in tow, shaking herself from white back to black. Never have I seen a dog breathe with such enthusiasm. And we are back by the cookstove again. I almost touch the surface with my hands. Snow from petting the dog melts instantly, slips in drops to the flat black plates, and hisses like a wild animal.

If I could only articulate the thing in the back of my throat. The necessity of stopping the flow of time. Of my plan to arrest the rapid succession of day after day. My plan is to lecture my two daughters: I'm sorry, but your mother and I have decided you are not allowed to grow up. You must stay like this for the rest of your lives. We are all going to stay just like this forever.

Outdoors, the pheasants arrive by the side of the old pigeon pen, where our two pet pigeons huddled through the dark, cold night: Rosa and Chez, waiting for me to bring cracked corn and fresh water. The male pheasant is scratching about in the snow, looking for the corn that is not there yet, the humbler female prancing about. Their feet leave beautiful delicate etchings in the snow and then the wind erases them, but the pheasants will come back to do it again.

And I am satisfied again that we are a long, long way from the shopping malls. I bundle up in my worst but warmest coat and pull the hood tight, tie it so it dents my chin, and gladly go out into the cold, booted, mittened, as warm as one can be on a day when wind drives reckless across the frozen lake and whips shingles from the roof of my house. The pigeons are glad to see me, and the pheasants hover not far off in the thicket of leafless wild rose, an old, dead, bent, and gnarled apple tree half-sheltering them from the blast. Cracked corn for everyone, the caged and the free. When the sun strikes away the clouds, I'll open the door and let my birds ascend into the heavens; but now an eagle, big as any bird I've seen, is cruising low, riding the wind south from far up the lake. When he finds the coast, he'll quit his downwind tour and make a slow, heavy tack north to find his mate. There will be mice to be had, despite the snow that hides them, but he will not have my pigeons today.

I walk up the hill among the well-spaced spruce trees, and put bare fingers into the snow to find two frozen cranberries, toss them in my mouth and roll them around like marbles, then walk on further until I come to the forest that steals the sting from the wind. The grey, wispy fungus known as old man's beard hangs from the trees, and star moss covers most of the stones. Snow stays mostly above, clinging to the boughs of green needles. If the wind shifts even two degrees to the east, the snow will become heavier, and bend as it builds up on these branches, breaking some, sparing others. Right now, it still sifts through where the big trees have not stolen the sky. It's quiet here, and deep. And I will not dwell on stasis or permanence, but go home and satisfy myself that it is two days before Christmas and there is nothing, nothing I am obliged to do with this day but live it for what it is.

The wind relents by eleven A.M., and my family spills out into the bright world. The dog rolls herself until she is a puffy, white cloud with four legs, unrecognizable except for the teeth showing in her mouth and the yelp of adventure. My two daughters and I go out onto the frozen lake, and after the usual warfare of putting on skates in the cold outdoors, we skate on a smooth, hard surface hidden beneath the layer of snow that muffles the sound of our blades. The ice stretches north for nearly a mile to where the geese, at least a hundred of them, have gathered in the open water. We skate without speaking over soft, white clouds until the wind begins to drop and Sunyata tells me she remembers this very moment from a dream she had last night.

And the geese decide just then that it is time to leave because there will be hunters this afternoon. They rise up into the blue sky and flow our way, headed towards the sea and on to their next nighttime resting place. We stop skating altogether and look up, deafened by their voices, then stunned by this other thing we feel from their beating wings. It is something that tugs at you inside. Something elemental that pulls you half off the ice and up into the sky with them. When they pass and we three look at each other, Pamela asks me if I felt something trying to lift me. I nod yes, but do not speak.

When the birds are gone, some new force of gravity makes us all lie down on the unmarked snow and leave an imprint of ourselves—arms outstretched, staring up at the sky. My daughters both immortalize themselves as angels, but I do not. I settle for leaving a scarecrow behind, the mark of a man with long legs together and arms straight out at his sides, faceless beneath an empty blue sky.

Eventually, we follow the long thread of our skated trail straight back home. Why not go another route, arc out across the ice? But there is something about seeing your own home there on the far hill, capped in snow, car buried in the driveway, the sound of your dog barking at the back door. Why is it that this makes you skate straight and fast when the cold has found your fingers and thumbs?

Small catastrophes of removing skates and putting on rubber boots with frozen toes before walking the final leg to the house. Red cheeks, cold fingers, a glove lost in the snow. And as we stumble, stiffened with numb feet, across the frozen marsh near the garden, it seems appropriate that I am the only one to fall through an air pocket into the little stream below, and scoop icy December water into my boot. My daughters are pleased to hear me howl, and I pretend to be angry, but, in truth, there's something invigorating about falling through ice when it grabs only a foot and an ankle.

Inside, I wade through the jumble of skates and boots and snowsuits. The kids have already retreated to another part of the house, to phone calls and books, and I pull off my wet socks and howl a second time as the pain of thaw sets in, then bang my big toe trying to put my leg into the mouth of the oven of the old cookstove that still sings. I build a fire in the living room wood stove: bunched newsprint, thin kindling, some splints of maple, and quartered logs turning quickly to flame. A brief pause of coffee and toast, then I find dry clothes and winter boots. I'm off again to walk alone to the shoreline of the Atlantic.

There are ships at sea, and sparrows clinging to what remains of last summer's sea oats. The dunes fall away beneath me as I arrive at the empty beach, where the sand has been bullied into the sea by winter storms. We are left with rocks, each covered with snow, and some with ice where salt water has frozen into caps and other odder-shaped hats that might have been fashionable in Napoleon's time. The sea ghosts of morning are gone but thin filaments of mist still lift from the surface and drift into nothingness in the diminishing breeze.

On the rocky reef beyond the shore, I see shoulder-high waves forming, becoming steep as they catch the offshore wind, leaping ahead of themselves to create immaculate hollow tunnels. Gulls swoop in low and nearly touch wing tips to the faces of an unbroken wave and then, somehow, as if drawing energy from the wave itself, arc back up into the sky, circle and then do it again.

On the shoreline, melting snow and ice give a pile of kelp and seaweed an otherworldly, glistening quality in the sunlight, like it is a monstrous, tendrilled sea creature, beached but still alive. I take off my gloves and lift a long belt of kelp to the sun before tossing it back into the sea. With my back to the wind, my face to the sun, it almost feels warm but when a sudden, belligerent cloud steals the light, I feel the haunting return of the sadness and loss I felt this morning.

I look west, to where the cliffs are magnified five times their height: illusory, massive, steep, and white. The sun soon regains its power over the sea, the beach, and the dunes, as I turn around to go home on this empty and extraordinary day, approaching Christmas on the Eastern Shore of Nova Scotia.

Was Christmas Ever "What it Used to Be"?

Helen Fogwill Porter

In this passge from A Christmas Box, *acclaimed East Coast writer Helen Fogwill Porter recalls her early memories of Christmas family celebrations in St. John's, Newfoundland.*

"Christmas is not what it used to be," we wail. "It's just a commercial farce. Just a matter of get, get, get, and buy, buy, buy, and the more money you spend the better. Christmas has been commercialized beyond repair. Ah, for the good old days."

I wonder if Christmas was ever "what it used to be."

Don't we all think of the good things that happened to us in childhood as the absolute ultimate in happiness? And won't our own children, in ten, twenty, thirty years' time, look back on the Christmases of the swinging sixties and moan that Christmas is just not what it used to be?

Children, after all, are the lucky ones. It's not their worry if we get all our cakes baked in time, polish off our house-cleaning, and complete our gift list. They just know that, come Christmas Eve, a kind of magic will transform the house that has been in slings for the past month, the shimmering tree will be in place, and mother will wear a smile again instead of that grim look around her mouth. We older ones forget that this will happen, but the children remember. And, cynic though I am sometimes, never have I been able to escape being possessed by that shining Christmas Eve feeling. It comes suddenly, and it doesn't last very long, but I do think that life would be much poorer without it.

Some of my most unforgettable Christmases were spent in that part of St. John's that doesn't really exist anymore. I'm talking about the old South Side, the little town within a town that vanished a few years ago to make way for harbour development.

Perhaps even more than the first snowfall, an important harbinger of Christmas in those days was the great paper caper. All the women were unanimous in the opinion that Christmas just could not be celebrated properly unless at least some of the rooms were freshly papered. There was no such thing as a living room then, or at least we didn't call it that. Some folks called it the parlour, others the sitting room, but by far the ma-jority referred to it as the front room, often shortened to simply "the room." Whatever it was called, that was one room that had to be papered. Housewives studied samples of patterns, made their decisions and then trudged over to make their selections. When the South Side women had money to spend, they didn't say they were going shopping, or going downtown, or going on a buying spree. They just said they were going "over," and everyone understood. Although we had to cross the long bridge every time we went to church, or to the movies, or to visit North Side friends, we never said we were going over unless we planned to go shopping. And that little word still conjures up for me visions of shops with long counters and high stools to sit on when your feet hurt, grocery stores where you could pick out your own sweet biscuits from big wooden boxes, and small ice cream parlours where the most delicious sodas in the world were made by tipping a bottle of Ironbeer over a scoop of vanilla ice cream.

But to get back to the all-important Christmas papering. Well, when the selection was finally made, including an appropriate border, the work began. First the old paper had to be taken off (in some ambitious years the room was stripped "to the boards"), but before even that could be done all the pictures and ornaments had to be removed from the wall, and this was usually a job for the children. King William of Orange, on his never-ending trip across the Boyne, was taken from his place of honour over the mantelpiece, all the mottoes were removed, and the china ornaments were put carefully away where they wouldn't be broken. When all preparations had been made, it was time to make the paste, for the wallpapers in those days didn't have the conveniently sticky underside that they have today. The paste was made from flour and water, and how they got the lumps out of it was—and always will be—a mystery to me. Talk about papering the parlour! In our house, you couldn't see anyone for paste! But somehow, sometime, the room was finally finished, and my elders' loud sighs of relief indicated to me that Christmas could come as fast as it wanted to now.

All the other preparations were made that are common to most people everywhere when Christmas is approaching. Cakes were baked, puddings steamed, and during the war, parcels were packed for the boys overseas, for there seemed to be at least one missing from every home on the South Side. When I was very young, in the early days of the war, I was angry at the Germans because we couldn't have lemon syrup for Christmas anymore. To this day I don't understand why, but I remember hearing my aunt, an expert syrup maker, say sadly that since the war started you couldn't get the proper ingredients. And the bought lemon syrup was a very poor substitute. The war's been over for a long time now, and I still haven't tasted that unforgettable homemade lemon syrup. I wish someone would give me the recipe.

Of course, most of the men on the South Side were more concerned about a more bracing kind of liquid refreshment. Even those who were very sober and sedate all year generally managed to persuade themselves that a "little drop o' stuff for Christmas" was different. The women, who considered the taking of strong drink an indulgence for men only, could usually be persuaded to take a small glass of port wine at Christmastime, and blueberry and rice wines, being homemade, didn't really count, although some of it had an almighty kick to it. The children had to be content with ginger wine, which was wine in name only. Although it nearly burned the throats out of us, we couldn't imagine a Christmas without it.

Sometimes I wonder how many of our family worries and irritations really touch our children. Since I've grown older, I've often heard my father speak of the time during the Depression when his pitifully small salary was cut again. But looking back, I can't even remember which Christmas that was, so it couldn't have been very different from any other so far as I was concerned. With the carefree selfishness of childhood, I suppose I didn't notice that his coat was shabby that year, or that my mother put a new collar on last year's good dress instead of buying another one. I had my new, frilled yellow organdy dress, though, and shiny black patent leather shoes. I don't think they wanted me to know how hard it was for them to find the money.

In the last few days before Christmas, the grown-ups seemed to lose their minds, muttering under their breath that this year things would never be ready in time, and shooing the children out of the way. By the day before Christmas Eve, with school, concerts, and most of the big preparations behind us, the tension eased a little. We called it Christmas Eve Eve. Many turkeys and geese, traditional gifts of employers to employees, began to arrive on that day, most of them delivered in horse-drawn carts whose jingling bells announced their arrival. Cookies and fudge were made then too, with mothers and aunts wearing out their brains trying to think of new places to hide them from ever-searching fingers. The men of the family were a little later than usual returning from work that night, but the women were much more understanding than they were at any other time of year.

When I try to sort out my feelings from that long-ago time, I think the strongest one in our house was: "If only everyone in the world could be as lucky as we are."

I don't remember if I ever heard this sentiment expressed in so many words, but it was there, as real as the Christmas tree, and it was shared by everyone who lived under our roof. We didn't have very much, just a tall, narrow rented house joined to a lot of other tall, narrow rented houses, but there was a spirit there that seemed to be especially prevalent at Christmastime. We were ordinary people, living in close proximity to a lot of other ordinary people, but somehow few of us ever felt ordinary. It's beyond me to explain why.

Nowadays, we often complain that people don't just drop in anymore, but wait to be invited. Sometimes, fearful that I've been painting the past in too rosy a hue again, I ask myself if they ever did just "drop in."

I can state firmly that on the South Side, they certainly did, especially at Christmastime. Christmas Eve was the men's night. Late in the afternoon, the callers began to come, some of them arriving while we were in the middle of our pork chop supper, without which no Christmas Eve would be complete. When this happened, my mother and my aunt would look at each other with resignation, raising their eyebrows and lifting their shoulders. But it would not do to make the visitors unwelcome. They were ushered into the resplendently papered front room, where newspapers were still spread carefully over the recently scrubbed floor. And there they would sit, and talk, and drink, and sit some more.

One Christmas Eve in particular, I remember there was one caller who didn't seem to want to go home. My mother, anxious not to be inhospitable but impatient to get started on the tree trimming, told him gently at one point: "Mr. H—, Mrs. H— will be wondering where you've got to." I'll never forget his rather bleary but unwavering eyes when he looked at her and said slowly: "You want me to go home, don't you? But I'm not going." Poor Mom, defeated for once, retired to the kitchen, and that night it was later than usual before the tree decoration was complete.

When we finally crawled into bed, it certainly wasn't to sleep, for then the visiting began in earnest. Groups of men made their way from house to house, increasing in numbers and volume as they went along. One night, after I had finally dropped off to sleep, I was awakened by what seemed to me at that time the most beautiful singing in the world. I crept out to the stairs and looked over the bannister to see a group of men in the hallway led by silver-haired Mr. Neddy Harvey, a gentleman if there ever was one. "O Come All Ye Faithful" was their favourite carol, and the roof almost fell off when they came to the line "O Come Let Us Adore Him." It left me with the feeling that they were really on their way to the stable to worship the Infant King.

Next they sang that loveliest of all carols, "Once in Royal David's City," and then my grandfather started an old song about England's valleys and hills in which the other men, most of whom, like him, had never seen England, joined lustily and tearfully. That was followed, naturally enough, by "Carry Me Back to Dear Old Blighty," and then somebody suggested "Eternal Father, Strong to Save." Almost everyone there had a close relative in the Royal Navy. The women joined in then, their work forgotten, and there on the stairs by myself, I sang too: "Oh, hear us when we cry to Thee for those in peril on the sea."

> *Who can describe Christmas Day?*
> *I don't think I'll even try.*

Christmas Eve is, and always has been, my own special time. During the week that followed the big day, visiting was begun in earnest; the women entering into full activity now that they could at last rest on their laurels. The time had come to sample the cakes of their friends, savouring the rich taste but nevertheless remaining convinced that their own were just a little better. We children kept a record of how many places we "had our Christmas," as we called it, and there was usually one day shortly after Christmas when we all felt a little squeamish. Then, the thought of plummy cakes, rich shortbread cookies, and lemon syrup would make us shudder. We were soon ready for another round, however. As one of my mother's friends used to say: "It's worth a bilious attack."

Well, that was what the Christmases of long ago were like; my Christmases at least. When Christmas was what it used to be. But don't you agree with me that today's children, whose tired parents are even now embroiled in the household tasks that have replaced papering and putting down canvas, whose Christmas lists are far from complete and whose heads ache at the prospect of the baking that has to be done, don't you agree that today's children are as far removed from their parents' problems as we were long ago? And that for those same children, who have to grow up just as we did and face a future as uncertain as it can possibly be, this very Christmas of 1969 might well prove to be that unforgettable one, when for just a few brief moments all was right with the world?

About the Contributors

Nova Scotian **Will R. Bird** served with the 42nd Battalion of the Canadian Expeditionary Forces in France and Belgium during World War I, and his experiences as a soldier deeply influenced his writing. His many published books include *Here Stays Good Yorkshire* and *Ghosts Have Warm Hands*.

Phyllis R. Blakeley (1922–1986) was a historian, biographer, and archivist. In 1982, she became the first woman to serve as provincial archivist for Nova Scotia. Her books include *Glimpses of Halifax* and *Nova Scotia: A Brief History*.

Born in Scotland in 1917, author **Alistair Cameron** moved to the Upper St. John River Valley in 1929 where he wrote several memoirs, including *Milestones and Memories* and *Aberdeen It Was Not*.

Lesley Choyce was born in New Jersey in 1951 and moved to Canada in 1978. He teaches at Dalhousie University, runs Pottersfield Press, and has written numerous adult and young adult novels. He lives in Lawrencetown, on Nova Scotia's Eastern Shore.

Norman Creighton (1909–1995) was born in Nova Scotia and lived for many years in Hantsport in the Annapolis Valley. As a writer and radio broadcaster, Creighton charmed Maritime radio audiences in the 1960s and 1970s with his popular broadcasts about Maritime life and the natural world. He also created the CBC noon-hour radio series *The Gillans*.

Wayne Curtis is a well-known writer living in Fredericton. He has written numerous books, including *Long Ago and Far Away: A Miramichi Family Memoir*. You can find him online at www.waynecurtis.ca

Trudy Duivenvoorden Mitic is the daughter of Dutch immigrants who came to Canada through Pier 21 in Halifax in the early 1950s. She successfully chronicled her parents' early years in Canada through her book *Canadian By Choice*. As well, she has co-written *Pier 21: The Gateway That Changed Canada*.

Bob Kroll has written for the broadcast industry for more than thirty-five years, including CBC radio dramas, television documentaries, and historical docudramas for Canadian and American museums. He is the author of *Rogues and Rascals: True Stories of Maritime Lives and Legends*.

Cape Breton–born humourist **Andy MacDonald** has authored five collections of memoirs, including *Bread & Molasses* and *Don't Slip on the Soap*. Each relates tales of his boyhood and adult years, told with his signature brand of Maritime wit.

Writer and CBC broadcaster **Linden MacIntyre** was born in Newfoundland and raised in Cape Breton, and has written a number of books, including the celebrated novel *The Bishop's Man* (2009), which was awarded the Scotiabank Giller Prize, and named the 2010 Libris Fiction Book of the Year.

Antonine Maillet was born in Bouctouche, New Brunswick. The author of over twenty-six novels and plays, as well as the recipient of thirteen honorary degrees, she became the first North American to win the most important literary prize in the French-speaking world, the Prix Goncourt, for her 1979 novel, *Pélagie-la-Charrette*.

Best known as one of Canada's most distinguished poets, Nova Scotia's **Alden Nowlan** (1933–1983) is also one of the country's most enduring novelists and short story writers. His impressive bibliography of works includes *Will Ye Let the Mummers In?*, *The Wanton Troopers*, and the collection *Bread, Wine and Salt*, which won the 1967 Governor-General's Award for poetry.

Michael O. Nowlan was born in Chatham, New Brunswick. He spent thirty-five years as a schoolteacher, most of them in Oromocto, where he has lived since 1964. He has edited or written more than twenty books, including the poetry collection *The Other Side*, and the Christmas anthology *The Last Bell*.

Newfoundland writer **Helen Fogwill Porter** has authored numerous books, including *Finishing School* and a memoir, *Below the Bridge*. Her novel *January, February, June or July* won the Canadian Library Association Award, and in 2010 she was inducted into the Newfoundland and Labrador Arts Council Hall of Honour for her literary achievements.

Evelyn M. Richardson was a Nova Scotian author who won the Governor General's Award for Non-fiction in 1945 for her now-classic memoir *We Keep A Light*, based on her years on Nova Scotia's Bon Portage Island where her family kept the lighthouse.

Saint John, New Brunswick's **W. E. Daniel "Dan" Ross** (1912–1995) was a best-selling novelist with over three hundred books to his credit. He wrote in a variety of genres, including Gothic fiction, and used a number of pseudonyms including "Marilyn Ross."

Born and raised in Newfoundland, and a long-time resident of Nova Scotia, artist and naturalist **Gary L. Saunders** is known for infusing his passion for the Atlantic provinces into his writing. He has published a range of non-fiction titles, including *Trees of Nova Scotia, Discover Nova Scotia: The Ultimate Nature Guide*, and the childhood memoir *Free Wind Home*.

Stanley T. Spicer was born into a seafaring family in Canning, Nova Scotia, and was educated at the University of New Brunswick, Acadia University, and Springfield College. He has written numerous books on the old days of sail, including *Masters of Sail* and *The Age of Sail: Master Shipbuilders of the Maritimes*.

Nellie P. Strowbridge is a prolific writer from Newfoundland and Labrador, and the author of numerous books including *The Newfoundland Tongue* and *Catherine Snow*. She is an award-winning poet, columnist, and editorial writer, with a special affinity for all things Irish, and has served as Writer-in-Residence in Cobh, Ireland.

Prince Edward Island writer **David Weale** has been collecting the stories and sayings of PEI for most of his adult life. His works include *An Island Christmas Reader* and *The True Meaning of Crumbfest*.

Publication Credits

Bird, Will R. "Granny's Art." *Angel Cove.* (Toronto: Macmillan of Canada, 1972), 63–74.

Blakeley, Phyllis R. "Early Christmas Customs in Nova Scotia." *Atlantic Advocate.* (December 1965), 25–29.

Cameron, Alistair. "A Woodstock Christmas Eve Long Ago." *Aberdeen It Was Not.* (Hartland: Hartland Publishing, 1982), 103–106.

Choyce, Lesley. "A Stone's Throw From the Sea." *Driving Minnie's Piano.* (Lawrencetown: Pottersfield Press, 2006). 45–51.

Creighton, Norman. "Recollections of Christmas Past—The Gaspereau Valley." *Talk About the Maritimes.* Ed. Hilary Sircom. (Halifax: Nimbus Publishing, 1998), 160–163.

Curtis, Wayne. "Lingering Melodies." *River Stories.* (Halifax: Nimbus Publishing, 2000), 103–111.

Duivenvoorden Mitic, Trudy. "It Had to Be a Fir Just the Right Size." *Nova Scotian.* (5. 51, 1986), 4–5.

Kroll, Bob. "The Gift." [Talking book series] *The Wonder and Miracle of Christmas Past.* (Halifax: Kroll Group Incorporated, 1993.)

Maillet, Antonine. Trans: Wayne Grady. "On Christmas." *La Sagouine.* (Fredericton: Goose Lane Editions, 2007), 29–36.

MacIntyre, Linden. *Causeway, A Passage From Innocense.* (Toronto: HarperCollins Publishers Ltd., 2006), 96–98.

MacDonald, Andy. "A Coal Miner's Family Christmas." *Bread & Molasses.* (Don Mills: Musson Book Company, 1986), 50–60.

Nowlan, Alden. "The Kneeling of the Cattle". *Atlantic Advocate.* (December 1967), 32–34.

Nowlan, Michael O. "This Is Our Willie: A Christmas Story." *Atlantic Advocate.* (December 1982), 41–43.

Porter, Helen Fogwill. "Was Christmas Ever 'What It Used To Be'?" *A Christmas Box: Holiday Stories from Newfoundland and Labrador.* (St. John's: Harry Cuff Publications Ltd., 1988), 62–66.

Richardson, Evelyn M. "Fall and Winter." *We Keep a Light.* (Halifax: Nimbus Publishing, 2005), 206–213.

Ross, Dan. "The Tallest Tree." *Atlantic Advocate.* (December 1964), 69–73.

Saunders, Gary L. "The Christmas Secret." *September Christmas.* (St. John's: Breakwater Books Ltd., 1992), 27–34.

Spicer, Stanley T. "Christmas At Sea." *Atlantic Advocate.* (December 1961), 33–35.

Strowbridge, Nellie P. "Father Christmas Unmasked." *The Gift of Christmas.* (St. John's: Flanker Press, 2006), 76–82.

Weale, David. "Margaret's Masterpiece." *An Island Christmas Reader.* (PEI: The Acorn Press, 1994). 61–64.